Elena Kincaid, Maia Dylan, and Sarah Marsh

EVERNIGHT PUBLISHING ®

www.evernightpublishing.com

Copyright© 2019

Elena Kincaid, Maia Dylan, and Sarah Marsh

Editor: Karyn White

Cover Artist: Jay Aheer

ISBN: 978-0-3695-0013-7

Elena Kincaid, Maia Dylan, and Sarah Marsh

CATCHING FAETE

Beyond the Veil, 4

Elena Kincaid, Maia Dylan, and Sarah Marsh

Copyright © 2017

Chapter One

"Shit, shit, shitty, shit!"

Erica froze as expletives began to sound from inside the nursery. It wasn't hard to make out the cursing, but the laughter coming from the other adult male in the room certainly added another dimension to it.

"Shut the hell up, Ben, and come and help me clean this shit up."

Erica heard the desperation in her mate Leo's tone, but there was a thread of contentment and joy that ran through it, too.

Although she wasn't entirely sure what sparked the cursing, she could absolutely appreciate the joy and contentment. These were emotions she shared. How could she not when she had Eylwén and Finwén in her life? Erica and her mates had been charged with caring for the recently orphaned twin babies by Alak and Aeron, the High Dorum of the Dark Fae, a race once thought to be extinct. Her life had taken a radical change less than a week ago, and now she couldn't imagine it ever going back to the way it was.

"Why do I have to help clean Finn up? I'm holding Ellie, and she's not needing a change right now, are you, sweetheart? No, you're not. You're dry and happy and sitting with your Poppa and laughing at Daddy, aren't you?" Ben's baby talk had Erica's heart swelling in her chest.

She sighed at the use of the nicknames Gabe had given the children. The day she and her mates had been named as the caregivers for these beautiful six-month-old babies, Gabe had stood before them with a happy glint in his eye. As soon as she'd spotted that gleam, she should have been wary, but she had been too besotted with the twins to care. Gabe then proclaimed that if he were to have two new pups in his pack, then he was "damn well going to make sure they had names he could pronounce".

"Because Finn just … well, he … *Gods!*" Leo seemed to gag, and Erica began to get an idea of what might have happened. "The smell! What in the name of all that is sacred has Aneena been feeding them? And how much? I find it completely unbelievable that such a small little body could hold so much."

Erica slapped a hand to her mouth in an attempt to hold back her laughter. She had once thought that ridding the world of Aelfric and the captain of his guard, the narcissistic Kheelan, would be the highlight of her life, but now that she had her mates and the twins, vengeance paled in comparison. Everything she had ever wanted was right here in front of her. The thought that she might never have had the chance to realize this dream and the happiness it brought to her and her mates had the laughter dying in her throat, and she sent another silent "thank you" to both of the Goddesses that had made this possible.

As an adult, she always knew that her actions would have consequences. Some would be good, while others, not so much. One decision she had made while desperately readying for the battle of her life had been to use her Goddess-given gifts to rid the Fae realm of an evil the likes of which the human and shifter world had never seen before. It was not a choice she had made lightly, and although at times since then, she had regretted it, it was more so because of the consequences she had to live with, rather than the decision itself that gave her pause.

The Goddess who had given her the gift of healing had also been the one who had delivered the devastating news that the darkness she had taken into herself to destroy Aelfric, had left behind a taint that would make it impossible for her to bear children of her own. So yes, although she and her mates, and the men and women who stood with them had rid the world of Aelfric, Kheelan, and the horrors that they would have dealt her people, she often wondered if the price she'd paid had been too high.

Shaking her head to rid herself of such thoughts, she stepped into the nursery. A noxious odor hit her as she stepped across the entrance. She looked over at Leo and couldn't hold back a giggle. He was dealing with a diaper blow-out of epic proportions, and her other mate was sitting in one of the rocking chairs they'd had made for the nursery, laughing his ass off.

"What on earth is going on in here?" she asked, omitting the fact that she'd been standing out in the hall listening. "It's almost midnight, and these children should be asleep."

Leo looked over at her with a pleading look. "Finn exploded."

Erica laughed again as she walked toward him,

gathering another pack of wet wipes April had sent through the veil for her. "Although I'm sure that's not entirely true, but from what I can see, it might well be appropriate." As she neared the changing table, Finn, who was dangling happily in Leo's hands, spotted her, making his little face light up.

The happy gurgles he made as she approached and the way he pumped his chubby legs in the air filled her with love for the little boy, and despite the smell that seemed to surround him, she leaned in and pressed a kiss to his little nose.

"Hello, my little man," she cooed as she quickly removed the soiled changing sheet, placed a disposal mat over half of the clean mattress, and indicated for Leo to lay the baby down. "That must have been why you were so restless after dinner. Aneena and I started the babies on solids, so I should have anticipated this."

"Love," Leo said in a dry tone as she swiftly cleaned the baby, "not even the Gods could have anticipated *that* situation."

She smiled as she slid a clean onesie onto the boy, who was rapidly falling asleep now that he was warm and clean again. She picked him up and placed him over her shoulder as she turned to look over at Ben and Ellie, sighing when she saw him cuddling the baby to his broad, naked chest. Ellie was fast asleep, sucking on her fist and looking for all the world as content as any child could be.

Tears formed in her eyes as she walked over to the crib and placed her bundle down on the mattress, patting his small butt when he appeared to be about to wake up again. She sensed movement behind her and knew that Ben was placing Ellie in her crib across the room. Once she was sure that Finn was fast asleep, she walked over to Ellie and leaned down to press a soft kiss to her forehead, inhaling that baby smell she loved so much before stepping back and pulling up the side of the crib.

She reached out and turned off the main lights of the room so that just their night light illuminated the nursery. It was a present from Gabe and Braxas and featured lights that moved on the ceiling and walls that looked like puppies and kittens playing. The Fae used electricity powered by nature—water and wind—but they had no outlets like the humans did. Fortunately, they had potions and magicians who were able to create a small water-powered energy source that connected to the nightlight, making it function.

Erica stopped in the doorway and turned to look back at her sleeping babies. The Goddesses truly did work in mysterious ways, she thought. She might not have had the pleasure of birthing the twins, but they were hers. She knew it with everything in her. They were hers!

"Come on, love," Ben whispered in her ear as he urged her to lean back against him. "Leave them to dream of all the mischief and grief they will cause us over the next few decades. Now that they're asleep, let's make the most of this time we have alone."

Heat swirled within her, and she nodded. They had been Mommy, Poppa, and Daddy all day. Now it was time for Mommy to get her some.

Chapter Two

Leo had gone on ahead to the bedroom and lit all the candles they had, creating a golden glow that made Erica look radiant when she entered moments later with Ben. The smile on her face when she looked his way still made his heart skip a beat, just as it had the very first moment he'd seen her. He would swear that if he didn't have a shifter's strength, the sheer joy he'd felt since bringing the babies home and seeing Erica blossom as a mother would have made his heart explode.

He couldn't have anticipated how two small little beings could instantly repair the gaping hole that had been ripped into their souls when the Goddess Allyria had told them the price they would pay for Alefric's demise. But here they were, starting a new journey together, albeit, this one filled with much less danger, and much more need for an endless supply of wet wipes, but certainly just as important as anything Leo had ever done in his life previous. They would love and protect these children, and they would raise them to be the kind of people who made both sides of the Veil a better place.

"You look so resolved right now, Leo. What are you thinking about?" Erica stopped in front of him to gently caress his cheek with her hand.

"Just about how lucky we are … and how *lucky* you're about to get." He leaned in to kiss her as he landed a quick smack to her jean covered ass that made her yelp and laugh into his mouth.

"Now we're talking," Ben said. He quickly shucked off his own jeans and stepped up behind Erica to unbutton her top, revealing her soft, perfect breasts. He gently pulled back her wrists, using her top as a makeshift rope to bind them behind her. "How do you want it tonight, baby?"

Leo could tell from the quick increase in her breathing that she was in the mood for something a little edgier than "sweet" tonight.

"Mmm, I think I know exactly what our naughty little mate is looking for, don't I, baby?" He cocked one eyebrow at her, and her eyes grew hooded as she bit down on her lower lip, indicating that she knew exactly the type of evening he had in mind. "Ben, get on the bed, sitting with your back against the headboard. You, my love, strip off those clothes for me, *now*."

Leo released her bound hands and watched as she followed his commands, his cock growing harder with every quick inhale making her perfect breasts shimmy in the soft candlelight. He quickly rid himself of his own clothes, and when she turned back to him waiting for direction, he kissed her slow and deep until she was panting, her arousal scenting the bedroom. He drew back and turned her towards the bed where Ben had been watching their kiss, his fist leisurely stroking up and down his shaft. Ben and Leo both knew how much it turned their mate on to watch them, and Leo pressed himself against Erica's bare back, pushing his aching cock down to slide through her now soaking folds, teasing her, but not entering her.

"Do you like watching Ben stroke his cock while he thinks about you riding him, baby?" Leo whispered in her ear, moving one hand up to cup a soft breast while the other slowly made its way down her stomach.

"Yes," she answered in a breathless whimper just as his fingers parted her wet pussy and circled her clit, causing her hips to buck. "Please…"

Her moisture was soaking his cock as he took his time, moving his hips back and forth. He pressed all the way forward, his fingers leaving her clit only long enough to reach further and grab the head of his swollen shaft in between her legs. He brought it back up to nestle between her labia, rubbing against the swollen nub, making her moan and wiggle against him. When her arm shot up and her fingers tangled in his hair, he felt the tightness in his own groin that told him if he didn't change course, he'd be coming all over her wet little pussy in a matter of moments, but that wasn't part of his plan tonight.

Leo placed a delicate kiss on her neck and reluctantly drew back from her.

"Get up on the bed, baby." His voice was thick with arousal. "I want you to straddle Ben while facing me. Give him a good view of that perfect ass." He smacked her round bottom once again for good measure and loved seeing the skin turn a rosy shade of pink.

The little minx teased him by taking her time as she crawled onto the bed, keeping her legs parted so that Leo could see her glistening folds beckoning to him. When she reached Ben, she lowered her head down to take his swollen cock head between her lips, sucking on it for a moment, before slowly turning to straddle his hips.

He watched as she settled herself very deliberately over Ben's hard shaft, his brother's hands moving to her hips to slide her along the length of him, bringing them both pleasure. They looked beautiful together, Erica's head back in abandon, her eyes closed as she savored the feel of her mate beneath her.

Leo grabbed the lube they kept in the nightstand and threw it on the bed next to Ben, and his brother didn't miss a beat as he grabbed it and slid Erica forward so that his shaft was resting against her ass.

"Give me your wrists, baby." Leo reached under

the mattress and pulled out the wrist cuffs they'd stashed there. He pulled them up and behind the headboard so that her arms would be above her head while the rest of her luscious body was at their mercy.

"I see you've been shopping without me." She purred as she offered up her hands for him to secure in the soft, padded cuffs.

"Who, us?" Ben tried and failed at making his voice sound innocent. "These were a gift. Gabe thought we might have some trouble getting some 'alone time' with the babes needing you and all. He thought we may need to shackle you in order for you to take a break."

"Our Alpha is ever the considerate man." Her response was thick with sarcasm, but her breathing had increased as Leo secured the other cuff and it left her open to his perusal.

"He is indeed. Now be good and relax, baby. Ben is going to prepare that sweet ass of yours … and then he's going to fill you up."

"Oh! And then what are you going to do?" Her breathy tone sounded the same as when she said their names right before she came hard around them. It sent a thrill down Leo's cock, making him grab his shaft tight by the base.

He could see Ben using the lube on himself and then working his fingers in to prepare her for his penetration. The very idea of what he was about to feel was moving him to distraction.

"Once Ben gets inside that tight little ass of yours," Leo began, "I'm going to suck on that pretty little clit until you come screaming around him, and then I'm going to slide myself into your soaking wet pussy and make you scream all over again."

"Oh, my!"

****

Ben was determined to hold off his release, despite the protestations of his cock. He held himself still inside Erica's ass until Leo brought her to a screaming ecstasy with his mouth. She bucked wildly against him, gripping him even harder as she continually spasmed. He held her flush against him—her back to his chest—until she finally calmed in his arms.

"I need to change positions," Ben said. He needed to be the one to move, to drive them all into their orgasm after remaining so still, and he wanted to see himself slide in and out of her beautiful ass.

As soon as Leo positioned himself flat on his back, Erica, without preamble, impaled herself on him. She threw her head back and bit her lower lip.

"My Gods, our mate is so fucking hot." Leo groaned as he watched Erica's reaction to their touch, and it made his dick even harder, something he would have thought an impossible feat just moments ago.

"Move forward, baby," Ben gently ordered her, using his hand on her back to guide her closer to Leo.

Her ass looked glorious up in the air for him. He inched forward and entered her slowly, letting her acclimate to the feel of both him and Leo. He loved when they took her together. Her body felt even tighter this way, and he was sure that this was also the way that all three of them came the hardest.

Ben began to thrust inside of her, pulling almost all the way out before plunging back in. He and Leo quickly found a good rhythm, although this position left very little room for Leo to do anything but follow along.

Erica's successive moans drove him to move faster. "Harder," she called out.

"You want it hard and fast, baby?"

She let out a loud moan in response, and he gave

her what she needed … what they all needed. He thrust faster, his strokes going in as deep as she could take him. The sounds of their moans and his flesh slapping against hers filled the room.

And before long, Erica shouted, "I'm coming!"

"Thank you, Gods!" Ben finally let go and roared out his release. Somewhere in the background, he heard Leo calling out Erica's name.

None of them it seemed had the strength to move afterward. They only managed to position themselves side by side in an exhausted heap of tangled limbs.

"Mmm," Erica moaned sleepily sometime later. "That was so good. Just what I needed."

"It's what we all needed," Ben said. It had, after all, been nearly a week since they had last made love, what with parenthood basically falling into their lap and all.

"Let's get some sleep while we still can," Leo suggested.

They all agreed, and Ben smiled widely at the reason for his suggestion. The thought of being woken out of sleep from a crying baby or two—*his* crying babies—actually sounded wonderful.

Chapter Three

Ben did not have to worry about being woken up in the middle of the night. He was already wide awake. He had managed to doze off for a few hours after he and Leo tucked Erica in, in between them, but a nightmare had jarred him wide awake.

The dream had started out quite pleasant at first. He was in the nursery with Erica, Leo, and the babies. They were all on the floor on a multicolored playmat, the grownups sitting cross-legged as the twins crawled around.

Then, the dream morphed into something horrific. Erica stood up screaming, "My babies! Where are my babies?" He saw himself as well as Leo frantically searching the entire castle, but Ellie and Finn were nowhere to be found.

He had awoken clutching his chest and then immediately run straight to the nursery to find both of his children sleeping peacefully. He let out a long harsh breath while running his fingers through his hair, clutching at the strands. "Just a fucking dream," he whispered.

When he was satisfied that the babies were safe, he walked back into the bedroom, grateful that the gift of foresight did not belong to him. Erica turned to him in sleep when he got back into bed as if sensing that he needed comfort. He didn't need to overanalyze his dream to understand why he had had it. As strongly as he felt that those children belonged to him, Erica, and Leo, the Dark Fae council had not made their final decision yet.

He lay there, with his mate in his arms, sleep eluding him as he thought back on this past week and what was still to come.

****

The trio had simply thought that they were going into the Dark Fae village to acquaint themselves with Fae brethren they had thought extinct, but not long after they had set foot there, the babies were placed in their care. The Goddess of the Dark Fae, Rysanna, had willed it so. Alak and Aeron, the High Dorum, explained that the parents had died in a tragic accident, though they did not go into detail. What they did reveal was that Aneena, Alak and Aeron's cousin, and the newest Dorum council member, had been the one to save the twins, risking her own life in the process. She was unable to save the parents, however. Their mother, Halarra, had been her childhood friend, and Ben did not need Alak or Aeron to tell him that Aneena clung to her guilt. He could see it written all over her face every time he looked at her.

"You're wondering why Aneena wasn't charged to take care of them?" Aeron had asked him.

"I am," he had replied. He had to be sure that there was no one who would suddenly decide to lay claim on the children one day. He had fallen in love with the twins the minute he had laid eyes on them, had known in his gut, despite not having any kind of seer abilities, that they were meant to be his, Erica's, and Leo's, but as hard as it would be to give them up before they even had them, it would be excruciatingly impossible later.

"I know it may seem antiquated in your modern times," Aeron began, "but my cousin is still unmated. Our instincts for parenthood work differently than those of humans, and she would be more of a loving caregiver to them, rather than their mother. And she already has a role to play in their lives as a Duva Matra." At Ben's puzzled look, he explained, "It means one who guides children. A secondary parental figure, if you will, who aids in the growth of a child."

Ben supposed it was similar to a godmother, but was satisfied with Aeron's answer. He also reassured Ben that there was no other claim to the children, but a meeting was in order to make the handing over the care official. It took a few days to convene a council meeting. What Ben thought would be a simple matter of signing some documents—after all, it was their own Goddess who had decided to place the babies with them—turned out to be a heated debate, and not all were in favor.

The two-story meeting place structure in the heart of the village looked very much like someone's house from the outside, the face of the building was comprised of inviting yellow brick, trimmed grass and bushes, colorful flowers, and a paved walkway leading up to an ornately carved wooden door. Inside, however, the small foyer led into a grand room with high ceilings and a candlelit chandelier. Instead of pews, there were rows of either cushy looking chairs or couches facing the front. There was no podium in the front of the large room, only more comfortable looking couches facing forward.

Ben, Erica, and Leo sat in the front row with the twins. Erica held Ellie in her arms with Leo's arms around them. Ben sat on Erica's other side holding Finn. He tried to tune out most of the arguing as Finn sleepily opened his eyes and looked at his surroundings.

"Ignore them all," Ben cooed to his son in a whisper. Finn let out a gurgle and then closed his eyes.

Alak and Aeron were still arguing their case passionately, as Gabe and his mates arrived. They took seats near them in support.

"Our Goddess has willed it so," Aeron declared to the crowd just then.

"Do you dare to go against her will?" Alak asked

the opposition.

"We cannot allow these Dark Fae children to be raised by *their kind*," Ben heard an angry woman shout. He didn't bother to look up as she continued. "Our Goddess is the one who separated us from the Light Fae. Did she not?"

"And with good reason," a male council member added. "They are selfish beings. Our children should be raised by their own kind."

"Selfish?" Alak roared. "That woman," Ben saw him pointing at Erica in his peripheral vision, "nearly sacrificed her life, and *did* sacrifice her ability to bear children in order to protect her people from a tyrant. Those men beside her are shifters, not Fae, and yet they nearly died as well for the Fae cause."

"The time for separatism to come to an end is upon us," Aeron said. "It is time for us all to band together if we are to survive what has been foreseen."

"I am inclined to agree with you, cousins," came a soft-spoken voice from the back of the room.

"Thank you, Aneena," Aeron said.

But it appeared that their cousin had more to say. "Though I agree with you about bringing our peoples together, including shifter kind, and I have no doubt as to the bravery and selflessness of Lady Eyrica and her mates, nor do I question their ability to be good parents, but they have no experience with our kind." Ben heard no judgment in her tone as she went on, only concern. "Our Goddess told you to bring the Queen and her Kings of the Light Fae here to the village so that we may begin to bring our people together. She told you to show them the babies, to place them in their arms, and then what? How can we be sure that this trio is the right choice to raise these children? How will they know how to deal with their gifts when they emerge?"

It was his Erica who answered, her voice barely above a whisper, but nonetheless sure in her response. "Because I already feel them in my very soul. They are our fate." And then, as any loving mother would, she leaned down and placed a soft, sweet kiss on Ellie's head, before doing the same to Finn.

"A trial," said a woman sitting in the back next to Aneena.

Ben turned to look at her and recalled her as someone who'd argued not necessarily in *their* favor, but in favor of the Goddesses' will, as she had said.

"A trial period to see if these three Light Fae can be parents to our Dark Fae children," she continued. "And someone to help guide and teach them about our ways. This person shall also act as a witness to their ability or lack thereof."

"That responsibility is mine," said Aneena.

Ben thought that was fitting for her to volunteer since she had a vested interest in the babies as their Duva Matra, not to mention what he had learned about her in relation to the twins.

"Very well," Aeron said. "A two-week trial." He gave the two earlier naysayers the stink eye, a terrifying look, effectively preventing them from protesting. "Our Goddess would not oppose this."

Alak then added sternly, "And if at the end of this trial period, these Light Fae prove themselves worthy, Goddess help anyone who tries to interfere with their family."

Ben was really starting to like these High Dorum.

****

Sleep would not be had for Ben tonight, he was sure of it. He gently rolled Erica over to Leo after he softly kissed her lips, and proceeded to the nursery. This time, he found Finn awake, happily making his sweet baby noises in his crib and kicking up his feet.

"Can't sleep, little man? Come, Poppa will tell you a story." He picked up Finn and then dragged one of the rocking chairs over beside Ellie's crib so that she could hear the story, too, even though she was still sound asleep. "I want to tell you about my people—shifter kind—and now your people, too.

"Once upon a time," he began, "and a long time ago, there lived a large clan of people who faithfully worshiped Gods and Goddesses—four of them, to be exact. They were Earth Gods who nurtured the land and took care of its people.

"And then one very harsh and horrible winter, the clan began to suffer and get sick, and they went hungry because they couldn't go out in the blizzard-like conditions to hunt. So they prayed and brought what little offerings they had to their mighty and compassionate Gods and Goddesses. They asked for help for their people to survive the cruelty of nature's elements.

"In answer to their prayers, the Gods and Goddesses spoke to the animals in the forest around the village and asked if they would be willing to help the suffering people. The animals told the Gods and Goddesses that they believed the clan was an honorable one. They never hunted more than they needed, and they had always been respectful of the forest and the animals they shared it with. So, the animals agreed upon one condition. The clan must join their lives to those of the animals, and spend equal time in their shifted forms to let the animal spirit be celebrated.

"And so, the next day, the animals chosen by the Gods to save the clan, arrived in the village and they each merged with a human soul mate, creating the very first shifters. Wolves, bears, and cougars were among the first to be created. This joining brought harmonious delight to the Gods and Goddesses. The clan was stronger, smarter, and thriving in a way they could never have before.

"Eventually the Gods and Goddesses chose other deserving clans across the world and other worthy animals, until the race of shifters was complete."

Finn gave a happy grunt at the end of the story and then grabbed Ben's finger in his chubby little fist. "You liked that, didn't you, my little man? I like that story, too."

Just as he leaned down to give Finn a kiss to his forehead, he noticed someone standing in the doorway. Aneena stood gazing at him with an actual smile. He hadn't seen anything but sadness in her eyes since the day he had met her.

She gave him a slight nod before she took her leave.

Chapter Four

"All I'm saying, is that it's more than just a little bit creepy."

Erica grinned at Ben's words as he continued to bounce Finn on his knee. The five of them were sitting on a blanket out on the grass in front of their home, enjoying the sun. Both children were awake, clean, fed and happy, and it was a rare thing indeed for both of them to be in that peaceful state at the same time.

"She's their Duva Matra, Ben," Erica reminded him as she leaned over to tickle Ellie's tummy, reveling in her giggle that had her heart melting. "Aneena has a responsibility to make sure these babies are raised right. She has to go back to her people and clear any doubt there might be that the three of us can raise these children as our own, but in a way that enables them to know all aspects of their heritage."

Leo leaned into her and pressed a soft kiss to her temple. Erica felt her heart stutter at the move and knew she would always feel like that whenever her mates touched her. "We know that, baby. It's just hard to adjust to having a houseguest that seems to watch us at all times and critique everything we do."

Erica made a scoffing sound. "Oh, she's not always watching us."

Leo reached out and hand and gently tipped her face back toward the palace. Erica saw Aneena standing on the balcony that led out from the main foyer and sure enough, her gaze was locked on the five of them.

"Now, that's just an awkward coincidence, I'm sure," Erica said quietly, despite the tendril of unease that began to unfurl within her.

Erica recognized the expression on the other woman's face. It was a look she herself had worn at times after the Goddess had told her what her actions had cost her. It was the look of a woman who longed for what she saw in front of her, a woman who yearned to be a mother. *What if Aneena wanted the babies for her own?* Erica felt a pain strike deep within her chest at the thought.

"Erica?"

"Baby?"

She heard the concern in both her mates' tones and knew they must have caught the echo of that pain along through their bond.

She smiled brightly at them both. "It's nothing, just a bad thought that jumped into my mind, nothing serious." Both men didn't look convinced, and she sent up a prayer of thanks to the Goddess above that neither of them chased her for an answer. She was just being paranoid anyway, she thought. After all, Aeron had already explained to Ben that Aneena would be more of a caregiver to the twins rather than their mother.

Determined not to let wayward thoughts ruin her day, Erica focused back on her family, and the rest of the afternoon was perfect. It was one of those moments in life that photographs would never do justice to. She still wore a gentle smile on her face hours later, when both her children were tucked up in bed, and both her mates were off running through the woods in their wolf forms.

She walked into the kitchen in search of some of the chocolate Corrine had left last time she had visited, and drew to a halt when she encountered Aneena. The woman stood in the darkened kitchen staring out at the night.

"Aneena?" Erica asked, and from the way other woman seemed to jolt back to awareness, she knew she'd roused her from deep thought. "Are you okay?"

"I apologize, Lady Eyrica," Aneena hastened to say, and Erica frowned as she watched the usually calm and unfazed Fae start to exit the kitchen as fast as possible.

"Wait!" Erica moved to block her exit. "Stay and tell me what's bothering you." Aneena's troubled gaze lifted to hers then dropped back to the floor. "Come on, Aneena. The babies are sleeping, and the boys are out in the woods doing their wolf thing. We're the only ones here. Will you not sit with me and tell me what has you so lost in thought?"

Erica watched as Aneena seemed to struggle with herself internally, and was disappointed when she shook her head. "No, it is fine. I will not allow my personal issues to color the reasons I am here."

Erica sighed. "Right. You're here to critique me and my mates on our parenting skills."

Aneena frowned. "Why do you say that as if that's something wrong? We are entrusting you and your mates with two of our most vulnerable. Would that not be the way things are done in the human realm? Or here in the realm of the light Fae?"

Erica winced. "Of course it's not wrong, and yes, it would be done here and in the human realm. It's just upsetting to know that those two babies, who own a large part of my heart and soul already, could end up being taken away from me. Can you understand what that would be like? To be given a glimpse of what was possible, to be given everything you ever wanted before you know what that might be, but then face the reality that it might be taken from you?"

A haunted look slipped into Aneena's eyes for a moment before it cleared, and Erica had a feeling that perhaps the woman knew exactly what that was like.

"I have had things taken from me, so yes, I can

understand some of your fears." Aneena's words were quiet, and she paused as if unsure of herself. "Lady Eyrica, do you have regrets from the actions of your past?"

Erica was touched that Aneena had decided to open up to her finally, and she tried to choose her words carefully. "I think everyone has some regrets, but we can only do our best to make our choices throughout our lives. There are never guarantees of which paths are the correct ones to choose. Sometimes, you may think that you've made the wrong choice, but fate will surprise you."

"I have regrets ... but I hope you are correct. Perhaps one day, I will able to see past them to my fate."

Erica thought Aneena would say more on the subject, but the woman looked thoughtful, seemingly lost in her head. She wondered, not for the first time, if it was the accident that had taken away her childhood friend that haunted Aneena—the accident that had left Ellie and Finn without their biological parents. Erica had discovered very little about what actually happened that day, other than the fact that Ellie and Finn were still alive because of Aneena, something Erica would be forever grateful for. She wanted to reach out and hug her, to offer her comfort, but Erica wasn't sure that Aneena would welcome that type of affection from her. The Dark Fae were apparently different about social etiquette, she had recently learned. The moment of sharing passed, and Aneena nodded, her face resuming its normal stoic expression.

"I am here for a few more days," Aneena said quietly. "I will do my duty to the children as their Duva Matra and to my people as a Dorum council member. At the conclusion of that process, the children will be with whoever will provide them with the rich and loving environment that they deserve. What their parents both wished for them. It still remains to be seen whether that will be here or elsewhere. But remember this, Lady Eyrica. Eylwén and Finwén will forever be Dark Fae. Do not let your desire to be a mother outweigh what is best for them and their future, because I can assure you that I surely will not."

With that, Aneena left the kitchen, and Erica took a shuddering breath. She honestly had no idea what she would do if Ellie and Finn were taken from her. She felt a wave of love sweep through her from her mating bond, and she embraced the warmth of her mates. She knew without a doubt that they would be heading back for her as quickly as possible having caught her distress.

She left the kitchen, all thought of a light chocolate indulgence gone, knowing that Leo and Ben would come directly to her no matter where she was. She walked back to the nursery and stood between the two cribs staring down at the sleeping babies, her heart swelling with love for them both as a single tear slid down her cheek.

Chapter Five

"I think you two beasties may have gotten more food on me than actually ended up in your tummies." Leo sighed as he stood from his seat in front of the two highchairs and went to rinse out the washcloth that was covered in pureed pears, along with his shirt and jeans, which had collected most of the mashed peas and squash.

He was still getting the hang of feeding the babies from a spoon. Bottles were certainly much easier to handle, especially once Finn had figured out that blowing a raspberry when his mouth was full of food made his sister laugh every time. Leo had to turn away more than once when he couldn't stifle the smile in response to his son's antics, more so when it was followed by the sweet trill of Ellie's irresistible giggles.

"What is going on in here?" Ben laughed as he walked into the kitchen, taking in the carnage. Leo was scraping the baby food out of his hair. "It looks like a food bomb went off!"

"That's one way of putting it, isn't it, squirt?" Leo looked back at Finn, who then decided to show Ben his new trick, blowing what was left of the food in his mouth all over the place, causing both Ellie and Ben to erupt in laughter. "Ben! You can't laugh. Then he'll think it's hilarious and do it all the time." Leo sighed in defeat.

"Well, I'm sure that Mommy will dissuade him of that notion soon enough. For now, let's get these two cleaned up." Ben reached for the clean washcloth that Leo held out and proceeded to wipe Ellie with it since she was the cleaner of the two.

When all the soft pink skin was finally fresh once again, Leo and Ben plucked the children out of their chairs and wandered into the living room. Erica was dealing with some Royal Court issues this afternoon, so Leo was looking forward to some quality daddy-baby bonding time.

They settled the twins on their backs under their favorite mobiles and watched as their quickly developing brains took in all the little toys dancing over their faces. It was so amazing to him how he could see them changing and growing every single day. *What a miracle babies are,* he thought.

Ellie started to fuss a bit, so Leo grabbed her favorite stuffed giraffe out of the toy bin, and her chubby little fingers grasped onto it as she cooed, as if telling it a story of her own.

It didn't take Finn long to spot the toy his sister was enjoying and with a furrowed brow, he tried to reach for it, but their little girl was having none of it. Ellie kept making her happy gurgling noises at the giraffe, completely ignoring her brother, who was now making quite a fuss.

"Where's your lion, Finn? You don't want Ellie's silly old giraffe," Leo murmured as he dug through the toy bin, looking for the stuffed lion that Finn took to bed each night. "It's not in here, Ben. Did we leave it upstairs in their room this morning?"

"I don't remember. I'll run up and check."

"Maybe I left it in the kitchen?" Leo jumped up and peeked his head around the corner into the other room, searching the kitchen chairs for the fluffy little lion. Seconds later, his hackles rose and Ellie's sweet little voice had gone quiet. He turned back and gasped as he saw only one baby lying on the play mat. Finn, now happily gurgling, the giraffe firmly in his grip.

"Ellie!" he yelled, his heart felt like it was up in his throat as he searched the room for her. Unless she'd spontaneously started to crawl, there was only one other option. "Ben! This isn't funny. Do you have Ellie?"

He heard his brother's frantic footsteps thundering down the stairs, and his mind knew that he hadn't heard anyone enter the room while he'd looked into the kitchen. Hell, there was no being on Earth or the Veil that could have moved quietly enough to sneak up on his wolf.

"What do you mean, do *I* have Ellie?" Ben's face reflected the same fear that was rapidly blossoming in his chest. "Where is she?"

"I just stuck my head in the kitchen, and then *poof* she was gone!"

Ben raised his nose and inhaled deeply, a look of confusion crossing his face, and then he quickly moved to each possible exit from the room and repeated the action. Of course, in Leo's shock and panic he'd forgotten to use his most natural sense to look for his daughter. He inhaled deeply himself, taking in the faint sweet smell of the babies' lunch, then the scent of his son, and then... *What the hell?* Ellie's scent was still strongest right where he'd left her, next to her brother on the play mat.

"I don't understand. I can smell her still right here." Ben reached out and gently laid a hand down on the mat, but still, there was no sweet little girl. "Her scent hasn't gone past any of the entryways into this room."

Leo looked over to where Finn was happily playing with the toy, seeming not at all concerned with the shouting they'd just been doing, which in and of itself should have seemed a bit odd, since they generally didn't raise their voices around the babies.

"Finn, do you know where Ellie is?" Leo cautiously asked his son.

Ben softly gasped when Finn stopped playing for a second, his eyes briefly looking to where his sister had been playing, and then he went back to ignoring them, chewing on the giraffe's soft head.

"Do you think … that Finn … that this is some kind of Dark Fae thing?"

"I don't know, but every instinct I have is telling me she's still right there on the mat and we both can sense that she didn't leave through any of the doorways."

"What should we do?"

"Well, I guess we should call in the reinforcements." Leo grabbed his phone and quickly dialed the one person he hoped could help them. "Aneena? We need you at the house right now. We've got a problem with the twins."

Ten minutes later, the young Dark Fae burst through the doors, looking ready for battle.

"Where are the babies? What's wrong?"

"In here," Leo called out from the den. After what happened, there was no way he or Ben were going to take their eyes off Finn for even one second.

Aneena walked into the room, and her head tilted slightly as if she was sensing something they could not see. Her eyes took in Finn, laying there happy as a clam, and then she looked around the room. "Where is Ellie?"

"That's our problem. I stuck my head into the kitchen for a moment to see if I could find Finn's toy because he wanted the one Ellie had, and then suddenly, she vanished. When I looked back, Finn had the giraffe, but Ellie was gone, even though Ben and I can clearly both scent her as if she hadn't even moved." The words rushed out of him. Leo tried to temper the panicked tone in his voice, but he was way out of his depth here when it came to Dark Fae magic. What if those members of the Dark Fae council who had opposed them adopting the twins had been right? Were they really prepared to raise these children? *Would* they be enough?

Aneena knelt down next to the spot that Ellie had last been seen. She closed her eyes and her hands hovered over the area. Leo watched as her brows furrowed for a moment, and then he was baffled as one side of her mouth turned upwards in a slight smile. She spoke low, a string of Fae words that neither himself nor Ben could understand, and then suddenly, just as abruptly as she'd disappeared, Ellie's sweet little body was right back where they'd left her on the mat. There was a surprised look on her face, and then she saw her toy in her brother's hands and her lower lip began to quiver right before she began to wail.

"Oh, thank the Goddess!" Ben scooped her up and hugged her tight, trying to soothe her.

"What happened, Aneena?" Leo had to walk over and touch the soft hair on his daughter's head, just to make certain that she was truly there. His heart was still pounding a fierce beat in his chest. He didn't want to imagine what they would have done if Aneena hadn't been with them.

"My best guess is that Finn's talents are emerging. It appears as though he phased his sister from this plane of existence just enough that she could not be seen, heard, or touched, but not completely, as you were still able to scent her presence." The Dark Fae eyed Finn speculatively. "It's quite a talent to have, but it will require a firm upbringing, to be certain."

Those words terrified Leo. Did this incident mean that Aneena was going to recommend the twins be raised by parents that could match the magic that was developing inside of these two children? He loved Finn and Ellie with all his heart, and he only wanted what was best for them, but that didn't mean it wouldn't tear him apart to have to let them go.

"We could, perhaps, place a binding spell on their magic until they are old enough to enter into instruction?" Aneena offered quietly.

He looked up at Ben's face as he took in the Dark Fae's suggestion, and then he looked at the faces of his children.

"No," Leo answered, "I don't want to bind their magic. It's part of who they are, and we will just have to learn how to deal with it. No one is placing spells on my children."

Aneena simply nodded once at him before taking her leave of the room. Leo had no idea what she'd thought of his answer, and he didn't care at the moment. He knew in his heart that he wouldn't let anyone take away any part of what made his babies special. Leo, Ben, and Erica had been warriors before they were parents. They'd defeated unspeakable evil and saved their people from enslavement. Surely, they could figure out a way to stop two babies from turning their lives upside down with a little magic? He supposed the bigger question was would the Dark Fae council still give them a chance to find a way?

Chapter Six

"I'm going to throw up," Erica said as she squeezed Ben's hand tightly. "They won't even let us hold them."

"It'll be all right," Ben said, placing a gentle kiss on her cheek.

Leo did the same to her other cheek. "Just remember, Erica, that none of this will be on you should they decide against us. I was the one watching her." His voice was a pained whisper. Ben could almost hear his heart breaking.

"No, Leo," Erica whispered back harshly. "You did nothing wrong and everything right. You two are the best fathers any child would be lucky enough to have." She turned to Ben and squeezed his hand again.

Their two weeks were up, and the trio found themselves once again in the Dorum meeting place, awaiting the judgment that could either seal their happy fate or crush them so completely, that Ben feared neither he nor his brother nor their mate would ever recover. Gabe, Braxas, Corrine, and April and her mates were there for support, as well as Ishaya and Graham. No one else other than the council members were allowed in attendance. While it was also mandatory for Finn and Ellie to be in attendance as well, Leo, Ben, and Erica were not allowed to hold them this time. Aneena sat up front with her High Dorum cousins holding Ellie, while Alak held Finn. Ben imagined the council members staring at their children, mentally looking for any damage they inflicted on the babies. *Assholes!*

He and Leo moved in closer to Erica and held her between them. She could not stop shaking as Aneena recounted her observance of them for the past two weeks.

The crowd erupted in laughter as she told them about the diaper explosions, all but the mated coupled who had sneered at them the entire first meeting. They sat silently shaking their heads, waiting to pounce on anything they deemed an infraction, and they got their chance when Aneena began her report on the incident of Ellie's disappearance and Finn's budding Dark Fae powers.

"Two weeks and already they lose a child," the vile woman named Rhana scoffed in clear disgust.

Her mate, Lomer, then added, "We knew they would not be able to handle the powers of the Dark Fae."

"Silence," Aeron warned, piercing them with a deadly glare. "You will respect these proceedings. Speak out of turn again, and I will seal your mouths shut indefinitely for your defiance."

The couple widened their eyes and shrank back in their seats. Ben could see that the threat was not an empty one and that it was well within Aeron's abilities to deliver such a punishment. Aeron then looked at Aneena and nodded at her to proceed.

"They did not *lose* her." Aneena rolled her eyes. "With their sharp senses, they were able to determine that Ellie was there the whole time." She took a deep breath. "The powers our Dark Fae possess are certainly ones that may be hard for the trio to manage."

Ben heard Erica suck in a deep gasping breath at Aneena's words. His own heart beat frantically in his chest. This did not sound promising.

"The wolf shifters were with the children at the time, but were at a complete loss of what to do, so they called me," Aneena continued. "I suggested that perhaps they could bind the twins' powers."

Loud gasps by the council members rang around the room, including Clementeen, the woman who had proposed the trial period, and it had seemed by her facial expressions throughout the proceedings thus far, that her support had been garnered.

Rhana stood. "I believe that I am not out of turn to speak now." She stabbed the air with her pointer finger as she spoke, and all the while her mate wore a smug look on his face. "To infringe upon the growth of these—"

Aneena interrupted. "They said no," she stated plainly, looking directly at the woman. As Rhana continued to stand, Aneena went on. "Actually, the shifters looked at me like they wanted to tear me limb from limb for even suggesting to put a spell on '*their*' children." Rhana took her seat. "And as I said, Leo called me. He knew full well that I would report this, and yet he called me anyway."

Aneena turned her gaze back to the front of the room, addressing all the members once again. "I read a human phrase once in a book I was studying about the inhabitants on the other side of The Veil, and it said that it takes a village to raise a child." She looked at Erica, Ben and Leo. "And they have one. They have the support of true friends. The people they govern adore them, and they have me to help guide them. I have pledged my life to these children as their Duva Matra, a binding oath I intend to keep, but I am not their mother. She is." Aneena pointed at Erica with her free hand. "I have seen the love of a mother shining through her eyes since the day I saw her with those children. I have seen her wear worry, and joy, and motherly pride. And them," she said pointing at Ben and Leo, "they are the fathers. I have seen them act ridiculous as they learned how to change a child properly, laughing at one another in the process. They went to great lengths to make their children laugh and smile, and even told them stories about their heritage as if imparting it to their children like it was part of *their* heritage as well. And I can say without a doubt that their unselfish and unconditional love for their children will always be at the center."

Ben couldn't help the elation he felt at this moment. He looked over at Erica to see tears of joy pooling in her eyes. Leo held a hand to his chest, meanwhile.

"Are you ready to proclaim your decision, cousin?" Alak asked her.

"I am," she said. "I have spent two weeks observing a *family*, and so I believe they should remain."

"And you faithfully agree to serve as the Duva Matra for these children, assisting in their education as well as serving your duty on this council?"

Ben knew this was the formality part, and truth be told, he couldn't care less what they were saying at the moment. He smiled widely as he looked at Ellie and Finn, both of whom were wide awake and looking around the room. He could have sworn that it was for their mom and dads, for *them*, they were looking.

"I faithfully agree," Aneena said. "I shall work out a mutually convenient schedule with the Queen and Kings of the Light Fae." She turned to Erica and smiled. "I also don't mind babysitting once in a while," she added with a wink.

"So it shall be," Alak said, passing his ruling.

"So it shall be," Aeron repeated. "If there is no cause for objection to address, then I would like to continue on to the final oath from—"

"*We* have an objection," Rhana said, pulling up her mate to stand with her. "I suggest you reconsider." Looking amongst the members of the crowd, she added, "That you all reconsider." Turning back to face the front, she continued. "Will *they* need a babysitter as well?" she spat, referring to Erica, Ben, and Leo. "As a Duva Matra, Aneena will no longer be in residence with them. A few hours a day, several times a week at best, does not prevent incidents from occurring the rest of the days."

Ben had had enough. He stood and faced the evil bitch of a woman. "And we are capable of handling any situation, even if handling means asking for help. Do you and your mate have any children?"

Rhana pursed her lips. "No, but I don't see how that is relevant."

"And I can see how you wouldn't," Ben said. He gave Erica a gentle squeeze to her hand, letting her know he'd got this. He felt the anger rolling off her, but the last thing they needed right now was for Erica to blast the woman out of existence, despite how much he wanted to see her do it. "I see a bitter, prejudiced woman, who cares nothing for these children, and a mate who only knows how to parrot her. I look at the other council members and can respect that they wanted us to prove ourselves worthy enough to claim these children as our own. Hell, *we* wanted to be worthy enough. The three of us will spend the rest of our lives proving ourselves *worthy* to be Ellie and Finn's parents. You and your mate are the ones *I* deem unworthy of looking out for anyone's best interest but your own." Ben sat back down as Rhana and her mate continued to stand.

And then the room erupted in arguments, all against Rhana and Lomer, except for whatever garbage Rhana was spewing back. Ben had had his say and just tuned her out. He tuned everything out until two loud cries erupted from the front of the room. Ellie and Finn became inconsolable, kicking their little hands and feet out. And then something amazing happened. Wisps of mist emerged from the twins, and they formed them together. The three images they produced out of them were that of two wolves and a smoky apparition of a woman with short, dark hair and blue, electrifying eyes. The sound of arguing had completely stopped.

Aeron spoke first. "I believe the children have made their choice as well."

Erica stood up when the mists disappeared, and the twins began to cry again. "Please," she pleaded to Aneena and Alak, who were still holding them.

Both Alak and Aneena came over to the trio and gently handed over the children to them. Ellie and Finn let out a happy gurgling sound before shutting their eyes in peaceful contentedness.

Alak then walked over to the nasty couple, who immediately took their seats again. "The decision is now final." His words were loud, authoritative, and deadly sounding. "If you have a problem with your High Dorum, feel free to take it up with the one who appointed us. Let's see if she deems the two of you worthy of speaking to, hmm?"

"We trust in our Goddess's choice," Lomer sputtered.

"Good, because as High Dorum, I relieve you of your duty to the council," Alak proclaimed to both Lomer and Rhana. "I no longer deem your counsel valuable to the Dark Fae. This is not the first time your prejudice for other races has come to light. There is no place in our Goddess's grace for those with such darkness within."

"You can't do that!" Rhana exclaimed loudly, an annoying shrill to her voice.

Ben watched Aeron roll his eyes, while Alak, looking like he was seconds away from strangling the pair, said, "You're right. The decision must be unanimous between the High Dorum. Brother?"

"Get out of my sight," Aeron said to them.

"There. It's unanimous," Alak said with a smirk.

Rhana curled her lip in disgust, and then she and her mate proceeded towards the exit in a loud stomping fashion while muttering what Ben could only assume were curses in their Dark Fae language.

Before they reached the exit, Alak added one more parting threat to the couple. "I suggest the two of you continue to live peacefully, lest you find yourselves being forcefully removed—by me—from the village."

Rhana and her mate finished the rest of their exit quietly this time.

Once they were gone, it was time for the final oath to be taken and then Ben, Leo, and Erica would be officially deemed Ellie and Finn's parents.

Aeron and Alak asked each of them individually to vow their bond of parenthood and all three easily answered in turn, "I vow it."

More wisps of some kind emerged from Alak and Aeron, circling first the children and then the parents, literally binding them to each other as a family.

Forever.

Chapter Seven

Mine. My children.

Even now, hours after the decision was handed down by Alak and Aeron, and Ellie and Finn were declared theirs, the thrill of it hadn't dissipated. Erica stood in the doorway to the nursery, watching her babies sleep, her heart filled to overflowing. She didn't have the gift of foresight like Corrine had, but Erica was damn sure of one thing. She would spend the rest of her life protecting, loving, and cherishing her children, and knew beyond a doubt that Ben and Leo would be right beside her doing the exact same thing.

As if conjured by her thoughts, but probably more by her absence, she knew her mates were making their way toward her. The three of them had fallen into bed in a hurry to love on each other for a long while after they had settled Ellie and Finn for the night, not only in celebration of their family, but also to revel in the love and emotions that bound them as mates, as husbands and wife, and now as parents.

"I think this is what our life is going to be like from now on, Leo," Ben said in a dry, but playful tone as he stepped up to her left and wrapped an arm around her shoulders.

"I'm going to have to agree with you," Leo answered as he took his place on her right his arm sliding around her hip, and she was nestled between her mates, just as the Goddess had fated it to be.

Erica sighed contentedly as she slipped an arm around each of the men and tucked her head on Ben's shoulder. "What are you to talking about?"

Ben pressed a kiss to her temple. "The fact that if our mate is not at our side—"

"Or in our bed," Leo added.

"Good point, or in our bed where she was supposed to be, passed out in sated bliss or at the very least reveling in the afterglow of our lovemaking, then she will no doubt be with our pups. Case in point, we find you here, staring at our children and watching over them as they sleep. So, Leo and I figure that that's going to be our lot in life. We will come second to our daughter and our son, and I for one am absolutely okay with that."

Erica grinned, tilting her head to look up at him. "I bet that wouldn't be the case if it were anyone or anything else that drew my attention."

Erica laughed as both Ben and Leo growled at her, Leo even going so far as to lean in and press a bite to her neck in mock threat. Her reaction to that was nothing but pleasurable. Her mates' growls changed, taking on the tone that told her they had scented the change in her body as arousal spiraled within her.

"I fucking love how you respond to us," Leo murmured against her skin, making her shiver.

Ben's hand slipped between the opening of her robe, and he groaned as his hand encountered soft, warm skin. "I think it's only fair that you get excited as quickly as we do. The scent of your arousal is enough to have my dick throbbing in need for you, but add the feel of your skin to the mix and I am seconds away from laying you across the nearest flat service and taking you. Hard."

Erica's heart rate sped up at that thought, and she felt her body tighten even further. "I think," her voice was a sultry mix of need and breathless anticipation, "that sounds almost perfect."

"Almost, love?" Leo asked as he gently swayed into her, letting her feel the strength and steel of his own arousal. "What would make it perfect for you, because you have to know that Ben and I live to give you what you want? What you need."

Ben rolled her erect nipple between his fingers making Erica whimper. "I want both my mates. Together."

Erica heard both her men inhale sharply a split second before her world tilted on its axis as Leo swept her up and into his arms. His mouth slammed into hers, and Erica felt his kiss to the very tips of her toes. Her mates never did anything by half, and when they kissed her, they poured everything they were and everything they felt for her into their kisses.

As always, Erica lost herself in the moment, and when she was aware once more of everything around her, she was naked, straddling Leo's hips as he lay back at the foot of their bed. Somehow, he had managed to take off the pajama pants he had taken to wearing when Aneena moved in, and she could feel the hot, smooth head of his cock pressing against her.

Breaking the kiss so she could sit up a little, she grinned down at her handsome mate, reaching between her legs to stroke his erection, loving the flicker of color in his eyes that told her his control wavered. There was nothing more powerful for her than knowing she had the ability to push her mates to the edge of their legendary control.

Leo groaned, arching back as she pumped her hand along his cock, just the way she knew he liked it most. "Don't play with me, baby. Take me in ... take me all the way in."

Heart beating wildly, she moved and slowly pressed the head of his dick to her entrance so that it easily slid inside of her. Unable to resist, she tilted her head down to watch him slip into her body. She rotated her hips as she took him all the way to the hilt, not stopping until she was settled completely against his thighs.

"Oh, Goddess," she moaned as she placed her hands against the hard planes of his chest and threw her head back, reveling in the heat and slight pinch within that told her she had every inch of him.

"So fucking hot, so fucking tight," Leo moaned, and she felt his body tremble beneath her fingers. "You had better hurry the hell up, Ben, or you are going to miss this round."

Erica continued to roll her hips in small, tight figure eights, enjoying the sensations the movements sparked in her clit. She heard Ben moving behind her, and then she felt his hand pressing slightly on her lower back.

"Move forward a little, baby. I want to make sure you are ready for me."

Erica moved to place her hands on either side of Leo's shoulders, her movements bringing her face closer to his.

"Hey," she whispered, her gaze locked with his.

"Hey back, my love," Leo murmured, lifting a hand to gently sweep her hair from her face.

Erica stiffened as Ben began to ply her body with the cold lubricant he was using. She bit her lip on a groan when he used it to gain entry to her ass. Her eyes closed on the sensory overload as Ben began to scissor his fingers within her, using them to ensure that when he finally took her, he gave her nothing but pleasure and that small hint of burn that always had her begging for more. She whimpered when he removed them, feeling bereft.

A few seconds later he was back. "Here I come, baby," he said sounding a little breathless, and Erica was pleased that he was just as affected by his attentions as she was. "Push out, that's it."

Erica groaned at the feel of him pushing into her body, the slight pinch and burn as he stretched her added to the sensuous heat of arousal that had been building within her. She held her breath for a moment, and then released it in a rush when he was finally seated within her and she held both her mates in her body.

"Fuck," Ben growled, the sound loud in the room. "I gotta move, baby."

"Yes, please! Move!" Erica cried out.

Ben withdrew, and Erica moved a little to give Leo some room of his own to maneuver, and then she was unable to really think at all. Ben and Leo began a steady rhythm, one that was completely in sync so that she alternated between being full and completely taken, to almost bereft at the loss of both of them. The room filled with their shared sounds of pleasure, and Erica could feel her release building to epic proportions within her.

It wasn't long until their smooth movements dissolved into desperate thrusts, both her mates pounding into her, reaching for their own releases as they hovered just out of reach. Erica keened as her body began to shake, poised on the edge of the abyss. Leo and Ben both slammed into her at the same time once again, and that was all it took.

"I'm coming!" she wailed as her body flew off the edge and a tidal wave of pleasure crashed down on her. Her entire body shook and shuddered with the power of her release, but she heard both men cry out their own pleasure and she felt them jerking inside of her, their own orgasms seeming as epic and turbulent as her own.

Erica felt her release peak again, and unbelievably she came a second time, and she simply gave herself over to it. When she was finally able to open her eyes and concentrate on her surroundings, she had no idea how much time had passed. The room was mostly dark, but the curtains were open and the light of the moon lit the room in a beautiful white light. She was cuddled between her mates, the light cover pulled up over all of them as they simply basked in the afterglow.

"Wow," Erica whispered in a voice that held a slight rasp to it.

Ben laughed softly from his place pressed against her from behind. "You can say that again, pixie. Every damn time we take you like that I think it can't get any better, but the next time we prove that it can."

Erica laughed with her men and sighed, snuggling closer to Leo's chest. Before Finn and Ellie came into their lives, Erica was happier than she had ever thought she had the right to be, but there was always this shadow in her heart that her men couldn't quite reach. That place in a woman's heart that belonged only to her children. When she had found out that her ability to have children naturally had been taken from her, she had thought she would never be able to fill that void. Finn and Ellie filled it to overflowing, and yet Erica knew that if the opportunity or need arose, she had more love in her heart for any that might need her.

As clichéd as it sounded, it made her happy to see others in her life finding the same happiness. April had Donovan and Jason. Corrine had her Alphas Gabe and Braxas. Their sphere of family and friends was expanding, and Erica loved it. There was someone for everyone. That thought brought the images of Aeron and Alak to her mind.

She had spoken with both of them after the proceedings that afternoon, and they had both seemed preoccupied. If Erica were a betting woman, she would have put money on the fact that the two were more than a little frustrated. With the discovery of those cuffs that had held Kat captive and the sword used on Gabe, both of which had been infused with some kind of Dark Fae black magic, they had a lot on their plate. But Erica had a feeling that perhaps the frustration they were feeling was more on the sexual side than anything. The thought of the High Dorum, all powerful and dominant, being fated to a woman who was probably more dominant than any female they had ever encountered before, had her giggling.

"What's got you laughing, mate?" Leo asked.

"I was thinking about Alak and Aeron." Both men tensed. "Oh, stop it, both of you. I love you with all my heart, and you are both the hottest things on legs as far as I'm concerned. No, I was thinking about the journey we have been on so far. We have more questions than answers when it comes to the Dark Fae faction that's causing trouble for all of us. Then you add in the fact I am pretty sure both men recognized Kat as more than just a beautiful shifter with a mean streak a mile long."

"You think they are fated?" Leo asked, before barking out a laugh. "Fuck, I hope so. Those bastards need a woman who can hold her own with them, not to mention the fact I plan to be in the front row with a big bucket of popcorn to watch that relationship unfold."

"Kat won't give in without a fight, for sure," Ben added, and Erica could hear the amusement in his tone. "Leo and I have fought and worked beside her plenty of times when we were Gabe's enforcers. She's a stubborn one."

Erica felt a shiver roll over her skin, and a small tendril of dread unfurled within her. A premonition of things to come perhaps. "And that, I fear, is what is coming their way."

The three of them fell into silence for a moment. Erica shook her head slightly to clear those thoughts. They were for another time and in the light of day. This time was precious, and it belonged to the three of them.

"Have I told you both that I adore you?" Erica kept her tone light.

"More than once, my love," Ben murmured, and she felt him press a kiss to her shoulder. "You are the love of our lives, the light to our dark and the mother of our children."

Erica felt the slight tingle of tears at his words.

Leo rolled so that he lay facing her, his gaze locked with hers. "When we first met you in that alleyway, when you were wielding your sword and fighting for your life and looking so fucking beautiful, you stole our hearts. When you fled from us in order to save your world, we felt as if we were chasing fate with every step we took to get to you."

Erica reached up to touch his cheek even as she reached out to lay her right hand along Ben's thigh. "Now look at where we are. Married, mated, fated, and parents to two beautiful children. Catching fate led us to this moment, and I thank the Goddess every day that she deemed me worthy of being your mate."

Erica had often thought of fate as a fickle beast who toyed with the emotions and lives of those it was destined to help. But now she figured the Fates knew exactly what they were doing. All they really needed was faith.

The End

FIGHTING FAETE

Beyond the Veil, 5

Elena Kincaid, Maia Dylan, and Sarah Marsh

Copyright © 2018

⤢•◆•⤡

Chapter One

Katrina Faraday saw the punch coming. She had a split second to decide. Step into her opponent and take the hit, knowing she would then be close enough to use her smaller frame and speed to better advantage, or dodge the impact completely. Considering how many opponents the big bastard of a bear shifter she was facing had dropped with one hit, she figured the latter would serve her better.

Using her cougar's enhanced balance and agility, she threw herself backwards, bending like a reed in a storm. The move allowed her to watch as the brute's fist swung over the top of her body. From the speed it was moving she knew she'd made the right choice. Straightening as fast as she could, using every bit of her preternatural speed, she threw her elbow toward his chin. Her momentum gave the move some added weight behind it.

Pain slammed through her arm upon impact, and

she reveled in the bear shifter's answering roar of pain. She leapt out of the way of his wild retaliation swings. Shouts of approval came from the people crammed into the old warehouse watching the blood sports taking place in the caged arena in which she stood. She was the underdog in this match, so she figured those who were cheering had bet she'd make it at least six rounds before being knocked out … or worse.

Katrina grinned when she saw her opponent spit blood on the dirt floor. "Oh, looks like I caught you a good one, huh?"

The shifter glared at her, and she could scent how close his bear was to the surface. "Everyone gets lucky once in a while, bitch, and I guess now was your moment. But this match will end like every other one I've fought. With me holding your body above my head, moments before I drop you across my knee. I will snap your fucking back and leave you to heal with the help of the men in the crowd who are all sporting hard-ons because of you."

Katrina didn't react to the taunt. She just shuffled to the left, light on her feet, moving with him as he tried to circle her. When she'd been born, her parents had high hopes for her as a healer for her pard. It made sense since they both came from a long line of healers and passive cougars. However, as soon as Kat could talk, and make her own preferences known, they thought perhaps healing wasn't the vocation for her. Then, when they met her cougar, it became crystal clear that their little kitten didn't have a submissive bone in her body. Katrina was as dominant as they came, save for the exception of an Alpha.

Her opponent charged her with a roar, and Katrina leaped into the air. She used the supple, flexible spine of her feline kind to turn in midair and drove her fist into the back of the man's neck. She'd hoped to snap it, perhaps giving him an injury that would give him hours of recovery time, but she had no such luck. The fucker had to have the largest, thickest neck she had ever seen on a man. All she got for the move was a grunt from him and a fucking sore hand.

Landing lithely in a crouch on the opposite side of the cage, she hissed at the sharp pain that flared in her side. She and big bear had been going at each other for a few rounds now, and he had definitely scored a few hits. But as she'd been protecting her head, the fucker had tagged her ribs a couple of times.

The bear grinned at her when he saw it. "Looks like I scored a couple good ones on you, too, didn't I, kitty? Seems a shame to bruise that hot, fuckable body of yours, but I got expensive tastes. The five grand on this match will keep me in booze and whores for at least a month."

Closing her mind off to the pain, something she had learned from her Alpha Braxas, she sent him a sardonic smile. "Wait, you mean a man like you, with all of this," she waved her hands up and down in front of him, "going on, still has to pay for a woman to spend time with him? What is the damn world coming to?"

The man's eyes narrowed, and she knew he would make a final run at her. This time, he wouldn't lead with his fist, and he certainly wouldn't charge her with his head down. Nope, this time he would come at her head on, and she figured it was going to hurt.

The bear roared again, the sound of it echoing around the arena and stirring the crowd into a frenzy. Then he confused the hell out of her by walking calmly over to her. She thought perhaps he would spar, so she threw her arms up to block and fire a few jabs in his direction, but once again she was wrong. He simply took the three jabs she threw and then wrapped his arms around her.

She cursed when she figured out his game too late. With the amount of strength he had, given enough time, he could crush her internal organs, break her ribs, and potentially her spine. Healing from that might prove difficult. She had to act fast. Reaching up with her hands—even as she felt something give on her right side—she dug both her thumbs into his eyes. She didn't stop when warmth flooded over her fingertips and the coppery scent of blood hit the air.

"Fuck!" the bear shouted, and the dumb shit kept going.

Gritting her teeth, she maintained her grip and pushed harder. When something gave way beneath her thumb, the bear cried out and dropped her. Making the most of her advantage and her grip on his head, she slammed her forehead into his. She shook her head to clear the fog that settled in and was relieved to see that the move had dropped the big fucker to his knees.

Now, he was exactly where she needed him. Dropping her hands, she took a step back, then spun, moving quickly, swinging her right leg as she turned and delivered a perfect roundhouse kick to his temple. It was a mix of her speed, strength, training, and the reinforced heel on her boots that had the big bastard dropping unconscious to the floor.

The arena was silent for a moment and Katrina thought the only sound she could hear was her own breathing, but then there was a roar of approval. Fighting to stay upright and not show anyone how injured she was, she walked out of the ring, head held high. She walked past the next fighters and headed straight for the lockers. The sooner she got to talk to the fucker she had traveled here to see, the better.

Katrina groaned as she pressed an ice pack to her throbbing forehead and laid her swollen left hand on a bed of ice. Her shifter abilities would take care of it eventually, but that didn't mean she wasn't in pain. Just then, the sound of *Star Wars* light sabers battling sounded, and she sighed. That was the ringtone she had assigned to her Alpha. Deciding to pull off the Band-Aid this time, she reached for her phone and connected the call.

"Where are you?" Braxas practically growled down the phone.

"And hello to you, too, Alpha mine," Kat replied with a hint of sass as she slumped back against the wall.

Braxas growled, and Kat could hear his cat in the sound. "I would have said hello if you'd answered your fucking cell phone the first three hundred times I called!"

Kat rolled her eyes. "Braxas, you've called a total of fifteen times."

"I'm finding myself to be uncharacteristically impatient with you as of late, so fifteen equates to three hundred," Braxas snapped back. "Now where the hell are you? You've been gone too long."

"I told you, I needed to—"

"No, Kat," Braxas interrupted, "this is not about you getting your head clear. I accepted that for a few days, but it's been almost a month since we fought Nyx and Zayden and their Rogues. Your head is as clear as it will get."

Kat sighed. "Braxas, you know me. I'm not good with large groups." Cougars were a private breed of shifter, and although they were staunchly protective of and loyal to their pards, they also valued their privacy and solitude. "Hanging in the middle of Wolfville doesn't exactly sit well with my cat."

There was a moment's silence, and this time when Braxas spoke, his tone was more man than cat. "Now that I can accept, but only so far. I think this has more to do with finding Nyx and Zayden than you will acknowledge. In fact, if I were a betting man, I reckon you're back at that damn cage fighting arena in Detroit. And if you are, then you're challenging any shifter you can, the bigger the better, and trying to get a lead on them."

With the worst timing ever, a wolf shifter by the name of Hatton, the owner of the bar, aptly named Blood and Tears, stepped up to her. "Here's the five-grand purse from that last round. That was fucking epic, Kat. That bear's going to be picking teeth outta his food for months after that last move. Oh, and I have some good news for ya. That hyena shifter you wanted to talk to? He's just stepped into the bar."

Kat closed her eyes as Braxas erupted at the other end of the phone. She pulled it away from her poor ear and pressed her hand over it to muffle the colorful words. "Thanks, Hatton. Let him know I'm here and I want to talk to him. Tell him if he leaves, he bleeds."

Hatton grinned, flashing yellow-stained teeth that highlighted a lack of personal hygiene. He handed her a thick envelope and walked off.

She took a deep breath then put the phone back to her ear. "You finished with your mantrum?"

"This is a dangerous damn game you play, Kat," Braxas growled. "We can't get to you quickly when you are so fucking far away. If you need back up, we can't give it to you, and that is unacceptable. Now you're about to face Santini without us?"

"Not Nyx," Kat was quick to say. "This guy was

one of the Rogues he tried to recruit, but he turned Nyx down. I'm hoping he can give me a few leads on where to find the bastard. Once I have some good intel, I'll come back and we can plan."

Braxas harrumphed an unhappy sound. "Make sure you do. I will expect you in two days."

"Two days," Kat agreed.

"And, Kat," Braxas said just as she was about to disconnect the call. "Come back in one piece, will you? You're important to me. To all of us."

Kat felt the stirrings of warmth unfurl in her belly. "I will."

Braxas was a great Alpha. He led with the head and the heart and always put the welfare of his pard before his own. He had taught her the art of diplomacy—which her mother had thought impossible for her to learn. The pard was everything to Kat, and she would do everything in her power to protect it and her Alpha. Everyone she cared about was back in Vancouver.

The image of two men flickered through her mind, both of them hotter than anyone she'd ever seen, built like they'd spent their lives in a gym, with bodies covered with tattoos that made a girl want to trace each one with her tongue. They were identical twins. The only difference between the two was that one had a goatee and one did not. They were also annoying, overbearing, sexist, and formidable Dark Fae with powers she could barely comprehend.

Kat growled, shaking her head to rid it of such nonsense and concentrate on the matter at hand. She grabbed her stuff and rammed it all into her backpack. She had to talk to a hyena about a jackass.

Chapter Two

Alak bolted upright in bed as a loud high-pitched scream sounded from somewhere in the house below him. He instantly grabbed his sword and charged down the hallway to the landing above the stairs, meeting his brother there, who had no doubt been woken by the beast's call as well.

"Did you hear it, brother?" Aeron whispered as they both looked down into the great room below. "Where is everyone?"

"I don't know, but let us be careful. We don't know what kind of beast is attacking," he answered. "It must be fearsome indeed to have made it this far onto pack lands."

Then he saw it. It was sitting right between the entrance to the kitchen and the great room, screeching its battle cry, the sound of it hurting his sensitive ears. Alak had never seen a beast quite like it, silver and purple, much smaller than he would have anticipated for the awful noises it created. How inept were these wolves and cougars at protecting their own lands if this sly creature could sneak into the very heart of their home?

"Alak! Lady Corrine is within its grasp. We must save her!" Aeron raced towards the stairs just as Alak noticed where the Lady Corrine was trying to hide from the creature's clutches by burrowing into the hall closet. "Don't let it touch you, brother. It feels like it's creating a vortex to another dimension. There's no telling which evil plane it is planning on stealing her away to."

"Aye, I feel it, too, brother." With a battle cry, Alak leaped over the banister to land directly in front of the vile enemy. "Lady Corrine, you must flee and save yourself! My brother and I will deal with ending this vile darkness!"

Finally, the Lady popped her head out of the closet, and she removed the coverings from her ears to look at them in confusion. The poor Lady was obviously overwhelmed with fright at being attacked in her own home. The beast made no indication that it feared their wrath, standing its ground, its own battle hiss as loud as ever. The body was see-through, and Alak could only imagine how horrifying it would look after it had taken its victims, its lash-like tail so long he couldn't even see where it ended. They needed to act quickly if they were to save the Lady and themselves, and with a mighty blow from his sword he cleaved the beast right in two.

Corrine screamed as the beast's magic was destroyed. A huge cloud of dust erupted, and the sounds of its death throes satisfied Alak that they would now be safe from its wrath.

"Ah, my beautiful Dyson!" Corrine yelled. "I turn away for a minute to grab the other head attachment from the closet and somehow you guys manage to kill a seven-hundred-dollar vacuum!"

That brought both Alak and his brother stopping short as she knelt by the now dead beast.

"Are you all right, Lady Corrine?" Aeron asked stepping closer. "We thought this vile thing was attacking you."

"Oh, for love of the Goddess." She slapped her hand over her eyes, which only confused Alak more. "It was just a vacuum! I was cleaning the floors! Do you know how hard it is to get wolf hair out of a carpet?"

Her tone had moved from agitated, towards that warbling, terrifying note that enters a woman's voice before she begins to cry, so naturally, Alak began a slow retreat. He was *not* good with crying females. No, that was much better left to Aeron.

When Corrine raised her head and those big blue eyes began to fill with tears, he cursed to himself, and of course, his brother moved to comfort her.

"We can fix it, my Lady," Aeron blurted out. "Can't we, Alak?"

"We can?" he sputtered out, taking another look at the machine now lying in a mangled mess at their feet.

"Yes, we *can*." Aeron gave him a dirty look as he gathered Corrine up and led her away into the kitchen. "Let's just get you some tea for now, okay, my Lady?"

Seconds later, the front door burst open, and Gabe and Braxas ran inside nearly colliding with Alak as he was still examining the mess to see if his magic could fix the beast.

"Corrine! What in the hell happened here?" Gabe stared down at him in accusation, while Braxas went into the kitchen to find their mate. Alak could only assume they had both felt their mate's shock and then upset through their mate bond.

"We were woken by the snarls of this beast and thought Lady Corrine was under attack," Alak said, shrugging. "Really, you should be thanking us for coming to your mate's aide while you left her unprotected. But she is upset that we defeated her 'Dyson'."

"First off, did you use a sword on a *vacuum cleaner*?"

"It was *very* loud, and we were sleeping…" Alak's mood darkened as he had to defend their actions. There were too many new things on this side of the Veil they had no understanding of, and it made him want to be back home in their village.

"Second, we did not leave our mate undefended. She's perfectly safe here. Most of us clear out on cleaning day because the noise from that damned vacuum hurts our ears, but Corrine loves that thing … or at least she *did*."

Well damn, now he felt kind of bad for destroying it. Lady Corrine had been nothing but kind to them since he and Aeron had been here, and he'd gone and destroyed her favorite cleaning pet.

"I cannot fix this." Alak sighed and looked back to Gabe, who wore a smirk on his face. "If it were a natural beast or object, I could call upon our magic to help mend it, but I don't know what these materials are made from."

"It's mostly plastic, but don't worry," Gabe smiled and took a small rectangle out of his wallet. "Plastic fixes plastic. Let's go online and I can have a new one here by tomorrow."

Alak had just finished watching Gabe place his order with the online merchant in his den when Braxas walked into the room, shaking his head.

"Corrine is so mad at you right now, Alak. She's considering placing a 'no swords in the house' rule."

"Truly?" Alak grasped the hilt of his sword protectively. He wasn't about to let anyone take it from him.

"Nah, I'm just kidding. Aeron is pretty pissed that you aren't back out there helping them clean up that mess though. In the meantime, Kat checked in. I think we'd better put in a call to the troops. She didn't find the hyena we're looking for, but she did get a tip on the place Nyx and Zayden have been getting these dark magic weapons from. She should be back by morning, so we need to figure out how we're going to deal with this."

Finding the source of the dark magic weapons had been the top priority given to them from their Goddess, but much to his dismay, a lead on the Shadow

Elena Kincaid, Maia Dylan, and Sarah Marsh

Market wasn't what caused a strange excitement to
unfurl in his blood. No, it was the news that a certain
golden female was to return tomorrow. They hadn't seen
the Lady Katrina since the night of the battle, and her
presence had caught Alak fully off guard to the point that
his mouth *may* have gotten away from him. He still
didn't know that he trusted her, but by the Goddess, he
knew that he wanted her. Which was only all the more
reason that he should stay away.

Chapter Three

Aeron had hoped that the next morning's wake up would be far less dramatic, but once again, he had been startled out of sleep, only this time it was to a surly man sitting at the edge of his bed, brooding.

"What in the Goddess's name do you think you're doing, Alak?"

"She's here."

"Who?" Aeron asked.

"Lady Katrina," Alak replied. His expression intimated that the answer should have been obvious. "She walked right past me without a word when I opened the door for her."

The sun had barely yet risen, Aeron noticed. He could have used at least another hour of sleep, but sleep had apparently eluded his brother. He decided to focus on that first and not the golden female for now. "Couldn't sleep, brother?"

"I saw a darkness in my dream, Aeron, one like I had never seen before."

"Aye, I saw it, too." Aeron got out of bed and walked over to the window. He felt the warmth of dawn caress his face. Darkness was natural. It balanced out the light, but the kind that he had seen, the kind that his brother was speaking of, was not the kind to be found in nature. It was born of pure evil, and Aeron feared where that darkness would eventually lead. "Our Goddess does not yet know how to fight it," he said, though she would have imparted that knowledge to Alak as well, Aeron knew. The fact that he, his brother, and the Goddess Rysanna herself, were still at a loss at deciphering the makeup of what they were dealing with was quite daunting indeed. How does one fight an enemy they do not know and cannot see?

Despite the threat they would soon be forced to face, whether they would be prepared to or not, Alak sulking at the moment had nothing to do with it. He turned to face his brother and couldn't help but smirk when the real reason for his brother's presence in his room dawned on him. "I've never known you to hide from anyone before, Alak."

Aeron continued to smirk as his brother's brooding expression was replaced with one of ire. "I am trying to avoid the spell she casts, Aeron, until I know how to better fight it. Do not tell me you are unaffected."

Aeron sighed and shook his head. Then he walked over to the dresser to change out of his nightclothes, giving him a few moments to stew over what his brother had just said. He normally preferred to sleep in the nude, but given the dangers lurking in this realm, no, in this very house, he thought it best if he were decent in case he had to spring into immediate action as the events of the morning prior had proven. When he was dressed, he finally responded. "No, I am not unaffected." He puffed out a long breath. "I do not think she has put us under any kind of spell, however."

Alak widened his eyes in disbelief. "No? You do not think perhaps she is part of that same darkness we have foreseen? I will ask our Godd—"

"I already asked her," Aeron interrupted.

"And what did she say?"

"Nothing." Aeron shrugged. "She said absolutely nothing, but she did wear a very satisfied smile, as if she knew a secret, but wasn't willing to share."

"What is she not telling us?"

Aeron sat on the bed and faced his brother. "She doesn't need to tell us what you and I already both know. What I am pretty certain I knew from the moment I laid eyes on Katrina." Images of the feline beauty danced in his mind, from her long blonde hair framing her perfect heart-shaped face, her seductive, dark golden eyes, fierce expression, to her long shapely legs. There was no doubt she was a warrior, dominant and strong, but he saw a softness and vulnerability buried deep within her that most people probably missed.

Alak stood, holding his hands fisted at his sides. "You cannot possibly think that stubborn, impolite temptress is our mate."

Aeron barked out a laugh. "You think the Fates would intend a docile female for us?"

He received no reply. Instead, Aeron sat back and waited for the maelstrom of emotions to pass through his brother as he paced the room. He'd stop on occasion, open his mouth, shut it, and then resume his pacing, until finally his brother said, "She doesn't even want us. I saw only contempt on her face."

"Perhaps it was confusion," Aeron suggested, though he felt an unfamiliar emotion, akin to a punch to his gut at the possibility of her rejection. He'd never thought himself susceptible to these kinds of feelings. He was not a man without compassion, desires, and emotions, but he thought and led with only his mind and he had always figured he could override any matter of the heart with his head. He wasn't so sure of that now.

"We should leave," Alak suddenly said, interrupting his thoughts. "We could work on unearthing this threat from our own realm."

"You know what our Goddess said, Alak. We cannot go." Light and dark needed to work together if they had any chance of defeating this threat.

"Then we must steer clear of the female for now. I'm not convinced she isn't casting some sort of spell on us."

"Afraid of her, are you?" Aeron asked tauntingly.

His brother harrumphed. "Though I am pretty sure she bites, I'm hardly afraid of a little kitten."

"Whatever you say, brother." Aeron got up and strode past him out of the room. He told himself that he was going down to the kitchen in search of some breakfast, even if he had to make it himself in that beeping contraption, but *not* so in the back of his mind, he hoped to have a run-in with a certain statuesque *kitty*.

He could try to stamp out seductive thoughts of her, like the ones that had occasionally crept into his mind over the course of the last month. He could try to fight the Fates and reject the woman they had deemed to be his and Alak's mate, but why fight a battle that he so badly wanted to lose?

Chapter Four

"Welcome home, Beta."

Katrina turned from where she'd been standing head first in front of the fridge, to stare at the wolf Alpha who stood before her.

She tilted her head in a way she knew was very catlike and stared at him, unblinking. "Alpha, you're looking better than the last time I saw you."

She'd found it surprising at first to hear Braxas had exchanged blood with the wolf Alpha, but she shouldn't have been. She'd known Braxas all her life, and the man never failed to help where and when he could. That created a slight problem though as now she was also Beta to a wolf. Something she never even thought possible.

Gabe grinned at her and slapped a hand on his flat stomach. "Funny how a hole in your abdomen can ruin your day. What are you getting there, Kat, a little milk before starting your day?"

Kat held up the glass in her hand and grinned. "Didn't your mama ever tell you that milk cures all that ails you?"

Gabe grimaced, staring at the milk with a look of pure disdain. "Nah, I can see how it is for you felines, but for a wolf, there's nothing a hunk of rare steak can't fix."

Kat took a seat at the table and watched as the huge man moved around the kitchen with ease. It was clear he was preparing breakfast for more than just himself, which would make it easier for her to update all of them at once. Just then, Corrine walked into the room with the smile of a woman who knew she was loved, and had been recently. She was followed in by Braxas, who by the grin on his face, told her it had been very recently indeed.

"Katrina," Braxas said, and she could hear the relief in his tone.

It surprised her when Braxas stepped in, pulled her out of her chair and embraced her. Kat patted him on the back awkwardly. It would appear the usually aloof cougar was picking up more habits from this wolf pack than she had expected. When he let her go, she was hugged by his mate. The Fae woman might have been smaller than Katrina, but she gave it her all when she hugged a person.

"So good to have you home," Corrine said as she pulled back smiling.

Home? Kat wasn't sure she knew where that was at the moment. Just then she caught the scent that had haunted her dreams for the last month. A second later, the doorway was filled with the image of the man who accompanied that scent. Or at least one of the two. He was huge and had to not only duck to clear the top of the door, but turn to get his impressive shoulders through the doorway. She had known it was Aeron before he'd even appeared. Most would know because he was clean-shaven, but for Kat, she would know by scent alone.

As soon as her gaze locked with his, she felt her body react to his presence, just as it had the day they met. She had recognized the two as her mates, but there was no way in hell she would admit that. Not when neither of them seemed to be in a hurry to acknowledge the bond she'd felt locking into place that day, and especially not when she had no idea of what deciding to mate with two Fae warriors would do to her previously, perfectly laid out life. She hadn't seen them coming, and Kat didn't particularly like surprises.

"Lady Katrina, it is good to see you have returned safely."

Damn it. Even his voice did things to her that were probably illegal in most places, she thought.

His twin stepped into the room behind him, his goatee really the only thing that visually differentiated him from Aeron. That and the scowl that seemed to always grace his handsome face whenever he looked in her direction. She had to fight the urge to flip him off as she took her seat at the large kitchen table.

"So," Braxas said as he took the plate from Gabe, piled with food, and joined her and Corrine at the table. "You're back, which means you've found something, so spill it."

Kat looked up at the two Dark Fae, who now held steaming cups of coffee and were staring at her. "You sure we can talk freely?"

The tension in the room rose, but she didn't drop her gaze. Both Aeron and Alak set down their cups, rising to their full heights.

"Lady Katrina," Aeron began, but was immediately cut off by his brother.

"You think to cast shade on us? Aeron and I have done nothing but help you and your brethren. We do not pretend to be anything more than what we are and have been truthful and forthcoming from the moment we arrived in this realm. Nor have we used dark tactics to achieve some hidden goal. Can you say the same?"

Kat stood slowly, allowing her anger to swell in her body. "That's the second time you have accused me of employing some kind of dark magic. You want to accuse me of being something, then you had better be prepared to back it up." She started to move around the table, ready to throw down with the surly gray bastard. She thought perhaps that might help to expel some of the pent-up energy just being around them stirred within her.

"Sit down, Katrina," Braxas snapped at her, and

she froze, the essence of his dominance locking her in place. She frowned when she felt another forceful spirit fill the room. There were similarities to the dominance that would roll from her Alpha, but much stronger.

"You do not speak to her in that tone," Aeron growled as he wrapped his hand around Braxas's throat. Kat had been looking right at him and Alak but never saw them move, but now that Aeron had Braxas, she was free of Braxas's hold, and Alak stood in front of her.

Protecting me?

"What the ever loving fuck are you two assholes doing?" Gabe snarled as he, too, rose from the table.

Fuck! This could escalate quickly.

"It's okay," Kat whispered, reaching out to place a hand against Alak's back. Kat felt him inhale sharply at her touch and thought she might be going crazy when she saw the tattoos visible on his arms and upper neck move against his skin.

Stepping around him, keeping her hand on his back as she reached out to touch Aeron and saw the same reaction in him. "He *is* my Alpha, and I was being a bitch."

Aeron turned to level her with a stare, his unusual dark gray eyes locking gazes with her golden ones. "I do not care. You may speak to us how you wish. My *brother* however, needs to take greater care when he speaks to *you*, and no one, not even your *Alpha* will speak to you with disrespect."

She could feel the tension between the two brothers. Clearly, Alak did not like to be corrected by Aeron. His displeasure was written on his face, but he did not contradict Aeron's statement.

Braxas had been growling for the past few moments, but cut off abruptly. "I did *not* disrespect my

Beta. Not that I need to justify my actions to either of you. Her role in my pard was earned the way it has been for generations. She fought and bled for it. But I *will* step in and discipline anyone in my pard when lines are crossed, and you will do well to remember that. Now take your fucking hand off me."

Kat knew that tone. When Braxas was about to go nuclear, he didn't yell. His tone turned to steel. "Aeron, let him go. I have news, and I think you and Alak might be able to answer some of the questions it raises."

She reached out and took Aeron's wrist, gently pulling it from Braxas's throat and the room drew calmer when he let go and allowed her to tug him around to take a seat at the table beside her. Alak took the seat on her other side, but he still would not look at her and she did her best to ignore how right it felt to be between them.

"Well," Corrine began with a smile, cradling her coffee in her hands. "This has been an eventful start to the day. Kat, why don't you carry on with what you wanted to tell us?"

Kat nodded and picked up her glass. "The hyena I spoke to in Detroit had turned down Nyx's request to go rogue and run with them. When I asked him why he turned them down, he eventually admitted that he was uncomfortable with the tactics they wanted to employ."

Gabe frowned. "That doesn't sound right. Why would a hyena be uncomfortable with strong arm tactics? They live for that shit."

"His concern was more for the weapons they were planning on using," Katrina said. "He wanted nothing to do with the stuff they were getting from their underworld Fae friends." Kat saw Alak and Aeron both flinch. She turned to look at one then the other. "Do you know about this Fae underworld he talked about?"

Aeron stared at her for a moment. "Were those his

exact words?"

Katrina closed her eyes for a moment as she thought back to that moment. "Not exactly. He said, and I quote, 'the shit from the Underfae was full of black magic, and that shit will fuck a hyena up.'"

"*Ellunhiyk!*" Alak spat out what sounded like a curse.

"That explains a few things," Aeron growled.

Kat shot him a pointed look. "Well, share with the class, because it explains nothing for us."

Aeron dipped his head in acknowledgement. "As you wish. The day of the battle for your return, we encountered two things from our world that should not have been here. The cuffs they bound you with, which inhibited your shifting were one, and the second was the magic-infused blade used on Gabe. If this Nyx and Zayden were in contact with Underfae then they would have access to weapons and magic that could create a problem for us."

"The Underfae are a scourge in our world," Alak said in a tone filled with disgust. "We have long thought their numbers to be so few that they lived isolated from all others for survival, having been mostly wiped out in the last war."

Aeron pushed back from the table and stood. "We will need to travel back to this Dee-troit and find this man you talked to. I will want to read his mind and discover everything he might know of the Underfae. It is my hope he may know where to find them and their trading post."

Kat winced as she stood from the table. "Do you think you can find this place without him having to physically talk?"

Aeron frowned. "It might be a little more

difficult, but I can pull the thoughts from his mind."

"Good," Kat replied as she carried her glass to the sink, "because when I cut out his tongue, I didn't exactly leave him in any kind of state to talk … or breathe without medical assistance."

"You took his tongue?"

She turned at Alak's question to see him staring at her with a look in his eye she couldn't quite read.

Kat shrugged. "Yeah. Bastard thought to fight back when I was convincing him to tell me everything he knew. He made a mistake during the one moment he had the slight upper hand by stabbing me in the side, but he didn't twist the blade for maximum damage. When I was pulling it out, he got a little handsy, then ran his tongue down my neck, and tried to bite me."

"That fucker tried to claim you?" Gabe snarled.

Aeron and Alak both turned grayer, which she was coming to see as something that changed with their mood. If she had to hazard a guess what it might mean, she would have to say they were pissed.

"I guess," Kat replied in a bored tone. "Maybe he figured if I were bound to him I wouldn't kill him? However, he attacked when my back was turned. He had no honor, and what kind of a dick tries to mark a girl in the middle of a fight? That's messed up. I figured it would be more insulting for him to survive than to die. Cost me more than half the purse I won that night in damages to the owner of the bar and for payment to make sure that bastard was taken care of, which was a lot more upsetting."

Kat turned to walk out of the kitchen to grab her gear. It looked like she was on the move yet again. Not that she minded that at all. It was that Alak and Aeron would be coming with her that had her heart beating a little faster.

Chapter Five

Alak watched Kat leave the room, and once again he cursed his foolish tongue. He was so confused by his reactions whenever she was near. It was as if his own body had betrayed him and was no longer under his control. He knew she had been in no danger from her Alpha, and yet he hadn't even realized he'd moved to put himself in between them, although, it could have been worse. Aeron's reaction to Braxas's words had been much more violent than his own ... for a change. It had shocked him to see his calm and level-headed brother threatening an ally over such a thing.

"You'll need identification if you're to travel to Detroit with Kat," Gabe said, his comment breaking Alak from his own thoughts. "I'll have Roderick do up a couple of fake driver's licenses, and passports."

Braxas suddenly looked thoughtful. "They may stick out a little. Call attention to themselves on a commercial flight. What about one of the shifter-run cargo planes instead?"

"What is a car-go plane?" Aeron asked, taking the question right out of his own mouth.

Alak had a feeling that these shifters were not referring to other planes of existence, and he imagined this "Detroit" village they were supposed to go to must be quite a journey away if they wanted to use some kind of transportation beast.

"Here, this is a cargo plane," Gabe said, holding out his phone.

Alak took the proffered device, which was now showing him a moving picture like he had seen on the television. The video showed an enormous beast on wheels moving faster than their trucks, and then suddenly, like a huge metal bird, its feet left the ground and it soared high up into the clouds—too high.

"Absolutely not!" Alak crossed his arms over his chest. There was absolutely no way that he would be putting himself in the belly of a giant mechanical bird. These shifters had already confirmed time and time again machines used no magic whatsoever, and therefore it seemed completely ludicrous to risk such a trip into the sky all on the whim of an arrangement of moving parts. If the Goddess had intended Fae kind to fly, she would have given them wings.

"I am in agreement with my brother on this," Aeron said adamantly. "I will not get into that *thing*. 'Tis not natural," his brother continued with a look of disgust. "The Lady Katrina knows where we need to go, and if she has a secure location and she permits one of us to access her memories, then we can create a transport portal to this Detroit."

"O-kay." Gabe rolled his eyes, as the wolf liked to do, and too often for Alak's taste. "I'm sure Kat can accommodate you, but we'll also need to do something about your … appearance. You can't be among humans looking like you stepped out of a black and white movie."

"Of course," Aeron answered right before his magic flowed over him, and Alak followed suit, letting his own magic flow and fold around him.

"Wow!" Corrine's words were soft in wonder. "I've seen you two do this before, and yet I am still amazed at the change."

Alak looked down at his now caramel colored skin and scoffed. "It will do, I suppose. We can maintain our glamor for however long this journey takes us."

"You might want to go pack," Gabe stated. "Roderick should be done with those identifications shortly." He nodded at them both before leaving the kitchen.

Alak downed the rest of his coffee and waited for his brother to finish his before leaving the kitchen. Katrina reentered the house with a bag slung over her shoulder just as he and his brother were about to head upstairs.

"I just ran into Gabe outside. He told me that you're planning to use a portal to get us to Detroit?" she asked in an uncharacteristically quiet voice. "He said you would need to access my memories to do that. I'm not sure how comfortable I am having you two rummaging around in my head."

Once again, Alak's back was up. Did she think they had no honor? That they would invade her privacy? Part of him knew he was being irrational, but for some unknown reason, this female had the capability to wind him up, and he did not know how to deal with that. Luckily, just as he was opening his mouth to no doubt say something that would once again offend her, Aeron cut him off.

"I assure you, Lady Katrina, we will only access your memory of the journey and location, nothing more."

She looked back at Alak, her eyes almost daring him to speak, but he chose to turn his back and go upstairs to pack instead. He could still hear her voice as he walked down the hallway.

"What is his problem?" she snapped

"Forgive my brother's manners. I am certain he does not mean to be rude. We're both a little uncertain of our surroundings and how everything is so different here. It's just taking some time for us to acclimate, but we *will* catch up."

Alak couldn't stop the roll of his eyes as he

lingered in the hallway listening to their interaction, to his brother's attempt at being suave. Good Goddess, only Aeron would turn an apology into an opportunity to court Katrina. In his mind, he could see the vixen's golden eyes narrowing at his brother's flirtatious tone, and the picture pulled a small smile to his lips against his will.

"Look, whatever you *think* is happening here, Romeo, isn't," she answered back. "That bullshit down in the kitchen was completely uncalled for. I'm not some fairy princess who needs to be rescued. I'm more like the dragon, and I will bite if you get in my way again. Never forget that. I'm a Beta here, and my job is all I care about. I'm not *looking* for anything else. You get my drift?"

Alak wished he could see her expression because her tone was overly aggressive in response to some harmless flirting. Calling his brother Romeo probably did not bode well either if she was referring to a tragic piece of human literature Aneena had told him about when she was studying human history.

A few seconds went by before Aeron finally answered. "Of course, my lady, I meant no offense."

"It's fine," she said, her voice strained. "We leave as soon as the IDs are ready. You'd better go pack your bags."

Alak quickly returned to his room and pretended he'd been packing the entire time. His brother's expression when he joined him was thunderous.

"She is stubborn beyond reason." Aeron grabbed the second travel bag out of the closet and began throwing clothes into it. "She attacks first, rather than share what she is feeling—kind of like *you*, actually…"

"Don't be angry with *me* because she rejected *you*. Perhaps that will teach you to apologize on someone else's behalf for once. I don't need you to fight my battles for me, brother."

"Well, between the two of you, someone will have to mediate. You're both rather ridiculous when it comes to being honest about what you are feeling. By the Goddess, I think it will take all the wiles and magic we possess to slay this … *dragon*, and claim her for our own."

Alak once again couldn't help the smile that appeared on his face when he thought about the luscious Kat claiming to be a dragon. Didn't she know? In the Fae realm, there was no one better to deal with dragons than the Goddess's own High Dorum.

Chapter Six

"What is so amusing?" Aeron asked.

As soon as the wolf shifter called Roderick placed the identifications in Gabe's hands, he noticed that the Alpha was failing miserably at trying to suppress his laughter. Braxas joined them almost immediately, and he, too, barked a laugh before checking himself. Corrine peeked around Gabe and shook her head.

She playfully walloped Roderick on the back of his head. "Idiot." She then looked over at Aeron and Alak and shrugged her shoulders. "At least these are better than the other ones I told him to redo."

Katrina, who had just stalked up to them silently, held out her hand for the identifications. She arched her brow, an act Aeron found quite sexy. "Richard and Peter Lipchitz." She glanced over at Roderick and asked, "Do I dare ask what the others said?"

It was Corrine who answered. "Moe Lester and Frank N. Stein."

The names sounded innocuous to him, even though the new set's surname joke was obvious and childish. He didn't miss the twitch of Katrina's lips, however.

"They're twins, Roderick. They can't have different last names."

"You're absolutely right, Kat," Roderick replied, beaming at her. "But at least I made you smile."

"Brother," Aeron warned. No doubt Alak had also noticed the way the wolf looked at Lady Katrina. His brother stood poised to attack. As much as he wanted to do serious damage to the jokester, he knew it would offend his hosts. As if sensing the tension, Gabe quickly dismissed Roderick, who with one last fawning gaze at Lady Katrina, departed. Aeron didn't bother denying his relief that she, however, did not return his affections.

"If we are done snickering over these silly names, perhaps we should go," Alak said.

When the three of them were finally alone, Katrina handed Aeron the *IDs*, as she had called them, and explained, "Richard and Peter are both names that are used to refer to the male appendage. And Lip—"

"I think we understood that part," Alak interrupted her. "Shall we?"

The three of them exited through the back and walked towards the forest to find a quiet spot away from prying shifter eyes. He and Alak would keep their word to the fierce little cougar and only pull what they needed from her, but however, the act would still be an intimate one.

"I never understood the need for surnames," Aeron remarked to fill the silence as they walked.

"It's an extra identifiable factor, like for which family you belong to," Katrina explained, "and there are billions of people on this side of the Veil. I suppose it's a good way to distinguish one Tom, Dick, and Harry, from the next." She paused for a moment before asking, "No one in your realm uses surnames then?"

"No," Alak replied. "We identify ourselves either by title, village, our parents, or even ancestors. Aeron and I are known as the High Dorum, sons of Areth and Arama."

Aeron was actually surprised at the information his brother offered Katrina. He was usually far less forthcoming and much more curt with those who did not already know their history. He was allowing her to know him, to know *them*, and Katrina actually looked interested as they walked and talked a little about their families. He learned that she came from a proud line of healing shifters, and despite following a different path from her family, the way she spoke of them, indicated that they were immensely proud of their daughter and her earned position in her pard. She took her role very seriously. What gave him pause to worry was the fact that he and his brother were both fierce protectors. He saw a willful stubbornness in her that would no doubt be unaccepting of their nature.

He decided to file that away for later, when and if circumstances would require him to think of it again. "What is your surname, Lady Katrina?" he asked to both distract himself and out of curiosity.

"Faraday," she replied.

Aeron took out the IDs. "Now that has a far more pleasing sound, I think." With a swipe of his hand, both forms of identification for himself and his brother were altered to read Alak and Aeron Faraday.

Katrina looked stunned. "Why did you need Roderick then if you could do that the whole time?"

"We have no use for that wolf," Alak stated with distaste.

As much as he agreed with him, Aeron ignored his comment, not wanting to incite anything that would disrupt their peace. "We cannot generate an object from thin air, especially one that requires these types of foreign materials. However, manipulating something already in existence is doable."

If she thought any significance or affront to him using her last name, she didn't say, nor did she show emotion in either direction, making him that much more determined to break through all the barriers she put up. The more he looked at her, the longer she was in his presence, it made his need grow for her exponentially. She was his and Alak's mate, and by the Goddess, he vowed they would claim her as such.

"We're here," she announced when they reached a clearing far enough away from shifter sight and hearing.

Aeron pointed to a rock for her to sit on, and when he placed a hand on the small of her back to gently guide her, she immediately stiffened. Though she did step forward, escaping his touch, he thought it was a small victory that she did not swipe his hand away.

"What happens now?" she asked looking up at him.

"Just relax," Aeron said. "Clear your mind and focus solely on the location."
They stepped up on either side of her and placed a hand, palm open, on her temple. "Close your eyes," Alak whispered to her.

Then he and Alak followed suit, closing their eyes and shutting out the world around them, all but Katrina. A swirl of large structures invaded his consciousness, much like the moving pictures found in this realm. Her mind kept jumping from one structure to another, to an elevated bridge with yet another type of mechanical beast, this one long, like a giant snake weaving and coiling. A *train*, her mind named it. Finally, she settled on a tall building, vehicles out front coming and going, travel bags being maneuvered in and out of the building. *Hotel*, her mind said. He saw Katrina's memories of talking to a man. He felt her anger as the bastard tried to claim her, her satisfaction of cutting out his tongue. This hyena was now a dead man walking for daring to touch his mate. He could feel the exact same anger and possession coming off Alak in waves.

This was it. They got it. The feel of this location, essentially, its essence, was now clear. He and Alak were already forming the portal that would take them there.

Just as he was about to break the connection with Katrina, another memory slipped through, one that had him horrified, a memory that did not seem much older than the one he saw with her and the now tongue-less shifter. He saw a type of enclosure. Outside of it, men were both cheering and jeering at the two fighters in the center. His mate was battling with a large man. She was hurt. He felt her pain, but she hid it well from everyone else.

He flinched from a particularly painful blow she received to her ribs, but Katrina seemed to welcome it. She felt alive and in control, and at the same time she wanted to hide inside herself until the pain disappeared, both physical and emotional. Despite being surrounded by people, and knowing she had her family to turn to, and her Alpha, who he could clearly see she looked up to and respected as a mentor and thought of as a brother, and who along with their entire pard, would gladly be there fighting beside her, she had never felt more alone. Images of being trapped inside a vehicle, bound, unable to shift, and feelings of complete helplessness also invaded her consciousness.

"Stop," her mind practically screamed at him. "Get out," it pleaded. "Please, just get out."

He and Alak broke the connection. They had kept their word, and only took what she had given them, but she looked angry for her apparent slip-up, so angry in fact, he thought she may punch the both of them.

"Lady Katrina, I … we did not mean to—"

"Would you stop with the Lady crap already?" she snapped. "It's Kat or Katrina."

"As you wish," he told her. He'd give her anything she wanted at the moment if it meant taking away her pain. He was wrong about her earlier when he thought she would never allow herself to be vulnerable.

She may be a fierce warrior, and her body may not need protection, but her soul was crying out for it.

He glanced over at his brother to see some of his protective armor that he built up against Katrina had been stripped. There was hope yet. For all three of them.

Nothing more needed to be said at the moment. He and Alak opened up the portal to Detroit, and the three of them stepped through.

Chapter Seven

"Um ... shit," Katrina whispered as her knees turned to water.

She'd been told the effects this type of travel would have on her, but wow, it sure did rock a girl's foundations. She would have dropped to the floor had Aeron not grabbed her. From the gentle way his hands gripped her shoulder and tugged her into his broad chest, she knew he had been waiting for that reaction.

"Take a few deep breaths, La—Katrina." She felt his lips move by her ear when he spoke, and she shivered at the sensation. A quick glance at the surrounding décor told her they were in an alcove, just off the lobby of the hotel she'd stayed in last week, and that they were alone.

Confused, and still furious with herself for showing them more of herself than she had planned, she pushed away from his strength, relying on her own stubborn will to keep her upright. "I'm fine. The sensation just takes a little getting used to, is all."

Aeron nodded, a small smile on his handsome face. "It can, yes. If I thought you would allow it, I would assist you through the portal so that you would not feel the physical affects as others of your kind do."

"What would that involve?"

Alak stepped in and answered for his brother, something she was coming to expect from the two men. "We would enter your mind as we did just moments before, you would submit to us, and we would wrap our own minds around yours to enable you to maintain your equilibrium."

Katrina shot him a look. "Yeah, that's not happening. Submission is not something I give lightly. You give a Dark Fae an inch and he takes a goddamn memory or two that he wasn't supposed to see." She held up her hand when Aeron seemed about to deliver an apology. "I didn't mean to accuse you. That wasn't your fault back there. It was mine. Let's just forget it and move on."

Grabbing her bag from where she'd dropped it, she moved out from the deserted area they had appeared in, willing her stride to stay steady. She walked up to the check-in counter, trusting the two of them to follow her.

"Katrina," Macy exclaimed with a huge grin. "So good to see you back!"

Kat grinned at the younger woman as she set her bags on the floor. "Yeah, I wasn't expecting to be back so soon, but there you go." Katrina had spent some time in Detroit over the years whenever her cat itched for a fight, and it was the staff here that brought her back to this particular hotel time and again.

"Well, it's always nice to—" Macy's voice cut off as Alak and Aeron moved to stand on either side of Katrina. "Well, *hello* to you." Kat heard a distinct change in Macy's tone and frowned. "Are you here with Katrina?"

"We are." Aeron smiled, and Katrina heard Macy's quick inhalation. "I am Aeron Faraday, and this is my brother, Alak. We would like to secure lodgings here in order for us to conduct business in this fine city over the next few days."

Katrina rolled her eyes. She was going to have to tell them to leave all the talking up to her from now on. If the two of them continued to talk like they'd both stepped out of an episode of *Downton Abbey*, then they'd be pegged as foreigners in no time at all. No matter what their new IDs said.

"I'm sure I can *service* your request just fine," Macy said in a syrupy voice that had Kat's inner feline growling with displeasure.

Alak turned a pointed look in her direction at the sound.

"We just need a room for a few days. Thanks, Macy," Kat said, and if Macy heard the clipped tone Kat used, she chose to completely ignore it.

"Of course. So is that three individual rooms?" Macy used that moment to lean forward, showing off her ample cleavage and looking up at Alak from beneath lowered lashes. The only thing that would make her appear more available would be if the words "fuck me now" were tattooed on her forehead. "We can give you the same room you had before, Katrina, and I can book your brothers into two king suites on the top floor. If you'd like, Alak, I can show you all the amenities in your room and make sure that *everything* is to your liking."

"They are not my brothers," Katrina spoke through gritted teeth.

Katrina felt the scowl on her face as she stared Macy down. Perhaps, she'd find a new hotel to stay in after all, she thought, just as she noticed Aeron glancing between her and her new skanky nemesis in her peripheral vision.

"I can assure you, Macy, that Kat is most definitely not our sister," Aeron said, "and we will require a suite for our stay. One that would accommodate all *three* of us."

Katrina shouldn't have enjoyed the shocked look on Macy's face at that announcement, but she did. A lot. She should have also insisted on having her own room, but she wasn't about to do that either—for reasons she wasn't prepared to analyze right at this moment.

"Oh! Well, I—I see," Macy spluttered as she started clicking away on her mouse, color rising into her cheeks. "The only room we have that would accommodate all three of you would be our Presidential Suite on the top floor. It is a lot more expensive than the standard cheap room you usually use, Katrina."

Kat didn't think she was imagining the pointed slur Macy had just thrown her way.

"I'm sure you'll find this will cover it all," Alak said with a growl in his voice that Kat would have concluded was his animal close to the surface had he been a shifter. Kat glanced down at the card he'd placed on the counter and had to fight to keep her jaw from dropping. *Where the hell did he get a damn American Express Centurion card?* Those things were invitation only, and you had to have serious coin to be invited to that particular party.

Macy's lips tightened even further, and she went through the motions of getting them booked into the room. "You're all set, Mr. Faraday. Any and all charges to the room will be placed against the card on check out."

Kat grinned at the woman, who was no longer trying to hide her sour expression. "Thanks, Macy. If you could arrange for our bags to be taken up to our room, we'd appreciate it." Without waiting for an answer, she turned back to the front door, pushed her arm through Alak and Aeron's arms as they turned beside her, and strolled out of the hotel.

When they were out on the street, she led them in the direction of the bar she'd fought in last week. Once they were out of sight, she withdrew her arms and sped up.

"Katrina," Aeron called as he and Alak simply lengthened their strides to keep her between them. "Were you perhaps a little jealous of Macy's attention?"

Kat frowned, refusing to acknowledge the warmth that had spread into her cheeks. *When the hell did I start blushing?* "Of course, I wasn't."

"You do *know* that we can sense a lie, Katrina?" Alak said in a dry tone.

Nope, she didn't know that at all. Rather than compounding it by acknowledging his comment or the heat in her face, she barreled up the sidewalk and tried to ignore the two men following her until they finally arrived at their destination. The dive they wandered into was tiny and only had a half-lit sign that read "Watering Hole" hanging precariously over the doorway. There were perhaps six bedraggled humans scattered throughout the space concentrating on their own drinks, and she could practically feel the confusion of the men with her as they stared around the room. The man standing at the short bar looked briefly at her and nodded as she walked past him to a dark hallway at the end of the room. She heard the click of the electronic lock the bartender had disengaged for them, and she continued onto their real destination.

Blood and Tears was strictly a paranormals-only bar that hosted an underground fight club. The ruling councils didn't like it, but they knew the consequences of aggressive species living amongst humans in a large city when there wasn't any safe location to blow off steam, so it was tolerated … barely. A smile spread over her face as she scanned the room. As luck would have it Hatton was standing at the bar. Kat would be lying if she said she didn't enjoy the way he flinched when he saw her. After all, what woman didn't like to be acknowledged for her dedication to a particular skill set?

"Damn it, girl!" Hatton placed both hands on the bar to glare over at her. "I can't have you back here so soon. I've already got that whining hyena calling for vengeance against you for the last time you were here. Do you know what that kind of shit does to my insurance premiums with the shifter council?"

Kat grinned as she slid into the bar stool in front of him. "Aw, come on now, Hatton. I know for a fact that you've earned enough off of me in the past to cover those premiums and then some."

She was aware of Aeron and Alak moving to stand behind her, and from the way Hatton's eyes shifted to them and back to her, she figured they were doing their intimidating scowl and glare routine.

"Ignore them," Katrina said with a dismissive wave of her hand. "They're with me. Now, speaking of that *whining hyena*, I've got a few more questions for him."

Hatton scowled, crossing his arms over his chest. "I'm not sure he's going to be too willing to answer a damn thing for you, girly. He's only just now able to communicate to where people can understand the fucker. Do you have any idea how long it takes to grow back a tongue? There's been a couple of his kind by here looking for you, too. There's a bounty on you now, Kat, and the value's high enough even I'm contemplating taking a run at it."

She felt the pressure in the room build and knew that Alak and Aeron were none too pleased with Hatton's words. She spun in her chair to level them both with a glare, ignoring the way her body heated at the sight of them looking all delicious and possessive with their eyes daring the man to make a move, and promising a grisly death at the same time.

"Chill the fuck out," Kat growled.

When neither of them looked away from a now cowering Hatton, she reached out and placed a palm on each of their chests. She inhaled at the shot of sensation that rocketed through her when the connection was made.

She pulled her hands away and stared at her fingers, sure that she would see them glowing or something.

"Katrina," Aeron said in a deep voice that had her cougar purring within her. "We can discuss the growing bond between us later. Let us just take care of this man who dares to threaten you."

"There was no threat," Hatton blustered, and Katrina turned to see him with his hands in the air in surrender. "I would not go after her ... I ... I mean, I was just joking—Kat knows I was just pulling her leg, right, Kat? She has no reason to fear me."

Kat shot him a look over her shoulder. "As *if*, Hatton. The only thing I would fear from you is a potential communicable disease from just being this damn close to you. Now, I know you wouldn't have risked getting the cage fighting shut down, so that hyena is still here. Let us talk to him and then we'll leave."

Alak leaned forward. "*Now*, little man. Before I lose my patience."

Once again, Kat's body surprised her as it reacted to the possessive, commanding tone they used. Goosebumps rippled their way down her body in carnal awareness. She'd always thought that because she had been blessed with a cougar as dominant as hers was, and the fact that Braxas was more brother to her than anything else, that she would never experience that shiver of delight that came when a woman contemplated ceding sexual control to a man. But damn if she wasn't seriously thinking about it now.

Chapter Eight

Alak guessed that the weasely looking male leading them up the back stairs was a wolf shifter, but he was weak. There was no doubt in his mind that he and Aeron could end him with just a flick of a wrist, no weapons or magic needed, and he would have in a heartbeat, simply for daring to threaten Katrina. There were two halves warring inside of him, one wanting to set the world ablaze in the defense of this beguiling female, and the other half trying desperately to remain rational as they fulfilled their roles as the Goddess's High Dorum. Never in his life had Alak battled with his inner demons as he was now. Primitive instincts clamored to be let out.

Claim her. Take her. Pleasure her until she screams her submission to us … until she knows who she belongs to.

He felt the scowl on his face as he followed behind Katrina and the male. His brother must have sensed the turmoil building inside of him. The expression on Aeron's face as he looked back towards him was concerned, and Alak forced himself to pull it together. It was humiliating for a Dark Fae of his power and position to be losing control like this—yet another reason to distance himself from the temptation Katrina presented.

When they finally stopped in front of a closed door, the wolf turned back to Kat and gave her a pleading look. "Now promise me you won't kill him, Kat. His sister rules the hyena clan around here, and if her boys come back and Dunc's had an 'accident' she'll take it out of my hide. You know how crazy those hyena females are."

"I promise, Hatton. We just want to talk to him,"

she answered honestly. "It's important. These orders come straight from Braxas. You have my word."

That seemed to mollify the older shifter, and he turned back to lightly knock on the door before using a key to open it. "Dunc, I'm coming in, but I'm not alone. Don't freak out."

The wolf's warning clearly hadn't worked, for as soon as they walked into the room behind him and the battered male on the bed got a look at Katrina, an awful noise began to come from the hyena's throat, and the stench of his fear filled the room. Alak had only encountered this particular breed of shifter once before during the battle in which Katrina was rescued, but none of them had made this kind of high-pitched noise, which sounded halfway between a whimper and laughter, and it was quite unsettling. Nyx, second in command to the Rogue leader, though not particularly bright, had at least presented the appearance of being in charge of his faculties.

"Get a grip, Dunc." Katrina sighed and moved closer. "We're not here to hurt you. We only want some answers."

"You won't hurt me?" His words were somewhat slurred, no doubt on account that his tongue was still healing from what Kat had done to him. The look that he gave Katrina was part fear and part adoration, though, and it was perplexing to Alak.

"Don't look at me like that," Kat snapped at the hyena. "If you hadn't tried to mark me while we were fighting, that tongue of yours would be just fine. As it is, you're lucky to be breathing at all."

"I'm a hyena." The smaller male just shrugged. "It's what we do."

"I'm well aware of how fucked up your species' breeding rituals are, Dunc. Like I said that's the only reason I didn't kill you. Now, we need to know more about these weapons that Nyx and Zayden procured. More importantly, we need to know *where* they came from. Do you know anything?"

Alak thought the male was going to answer her, but then he finally noticed the two of them standing behind Kat and the male cowered at the glare Alak threw his way.

Then he spoke. "Nyx wanted a meeting with my sister, Melanie. That's why he sought me out. She runs her clan pretty tight in this city, and he knew if he could get her support then the other hyena queens would follow. He and Zayden…" The hyena's eyes widened in fear for a moment. "They're crazy. Especially the tiger." His body shuddered.

"Yes, unfortunately, we've already had a run-in with them at home," Kat answered quietly. "So did your sister meet with Nyx?"

"She sure did. Mel ain't someone to pass on an opportunity, and we'd heard through the grapevine that they had some kind of magical weapons. She even went with that crazy bastard to see where he got these weapons, but when she came back…" Another shudder. "Let me tell you, Mel ain't one prone to exaggeration, but she said that Nyx had sold his soul to demons and that she was certain that the Goddess would forsake us all if we joined in with him. She said she wasn't going to bargain with monsters, and she told him not to return to our territory."

"That's the term she used … 'monsters'?" Aeron asked.

"Yup, she said they were unlike anything she'd ever seen, horribly disfigured creatures with vast amounts of dark magic. Nyx took her through some kind of portal. I don't know exactly where. She wouldn't tell any of us. But she did forbid any of the clan from traveling to your city."

"The portal is in Vancouver?" Kat's surprise matched his own. The portal to the market had been right in Gabe's backyard all this time. These rogues were bold enemies indeed.

"I overheard Mel telling our other sister that they went to that big park in the middle of the city. She was shocked the humans didn't stumble upon it until she went in and saw the extent of the dark magic being used to hide it from plain sight." Dunc paused for a moment, and then shook his head. "I don't think I've ever seen my sister actually scared of anything before, but these *things*, these monsters, they scared her good."

Alak could almost see the fury igniting within Katrina as the male's words sank in. The enemy had been making themselves right at home in Gabe and Braxas's territory all this time, right under their noses.

"Those bastards! They could expose us all to the humans. No wonder Mel was afraid of them starting a war. If we don't shut this down, it could very well happen."

"It's more than just exposure they want," Aeron stated, echoing Alak's own conclusion.

"Frederych and his experiments," Katrina whispered.

"Precisely." Alak and Aeron had had lengthy discussions with their Goddess about the traitor's actions, and his motivations were now becoming clear. He was working with them—the *monsters*. They wanted to enslave the humans.

Katrina's aggression was beginning to leak out. Alak was now familiar with the scent and the hyena shifter was getting nervous again as he eyed her from his perch on the bed, but there was something else mixed in with the smell of his anxiety—*is that arousal?*

Katrina must have scented it the same time as he did, because she swung around, pinning the strange shifter with a glare.

"Good Goddess, Dunc. Cut that shit out! You hyenas are so messed up. Keep on looking at me like that and I might take that tongue out for good."

"You're such an aggressive female. I can't help it."

The hyena appeared scared and hopeful at the same time. It was obvious this male was no threat to Katrina—her disgust was clear—but Alak found it offensive nonetheless that any male would attempt to court his female right in front of him and Aeron. The possessive fury was once again building to a rage inside of him.

"Well I suggest you *do* help it, or my brother and I will make certain that you can't assault another female *ever* again." Alak crossed his arms over his chest and let his glamor slip just enough so that Dunc could see they weren't to be messed with.

"What *are* you?" Dunc whispered as his face went deathly pale, and Alak's anger was placated when he cowered away, no longer looking in the direction of his female.

Katrina turned just in time to see the flash of their true skin color, and the expression on her face said she clearly wasn't pleased.

"What are you *doing*? Is this you keeping a low profile?" she hissed at him, then looked over to Aeron, who shrugged.

Thanks for the backup, brother.

"He was out of line. He deserves more than a

fright for what he tried to do to you when you were last here." Alak's anger was feeding off of hers, and even though he had a feeling his mouth was getting away from him again, Alak couldn't stop the words from tumbling from his lips. "I cannot decide if you are extremely brave or extremely reckless, putting yourself in a cage fight here with males three times your size. And then picking a fight with this miscreant straight after when you are still injured and could have been forcefully mated. How can Braxas let you run amok alone and unprotected?"

His voice was almost a yell by the time he was done, and as soon as he'd closed his mouth, he knew he had made a mistake.

"Oh, brother…"

Alak felt the resignation to the approaching onslaught in Aeron's quiet voice.

By the Goddess, the raw and potent rage he saw in Katrina's golden eyes as she stood before him, her fists clenched, and her body tight in anger, made his cock hard to an almost painful state of want for her. She was magnificent. She was also an active volcano he had just awoken with his very foolish words.

Some thoughts he was *clearly* going to have to learn to just keep to himself if he intended to survive the courtship of their dragon.

Chapter Nine

"Out … now," Katrina said through gritted teeth, inclining her head towards the door, her golden cheeks tingeing with a flushed bloom. Her eyes were wild as she looked from Alak to Aeron.

Aeron steeled himself for the tirade that would follow them out into the hallway, but not before imparting a few words to the once again cowering hyena shifter before he left. "It would be better for your health," he began, "if you never crossed paths with Katrina again." The extent of his mercy was allowing the hyena to live *this* time. He would not suffer such an affront to Katrina again.

His message was received loud and clear.

He and Alak both left the room, followed closely by Katrina. When he turned to face her, expecting the shouting match to begin, she nearly walked right into him, only angering her further. And yet, other than a growl, one he found sexy as sin, nothing else escaped her lips. She forcefully brushed against his shoulder, and she walked past him and Alak. He and his brother exchanged confused looks and then followed their fierce little warrior back to the bar and out onto the street.

The silence continued all the way back to the room they would be staying in, but as soon as the door was shut, Katrina, still red-faced, with her hands on her hips, began to speak. "Open up that portal. It's time to go." Her words were quiet, deadly sounding, not at all what he had been expecting from her at that moment.

"I do not think that's wise," Aeron stated. "This mission is not complete. We have learned much, but speaking to Melanie and gathering information about her experience firsthand should be our next step."

"And I intend to do just that," Katrina said, this time raising her voice. "I neither need, nor want, the two of you here. Your Vulcan mind-meld wasn't required after all since Dunc regained his speech, and I'm pretty sure that Mel still has her tongue."

"Who is this Vul-can?" Aeron asked, just as Alak said, "We are not going anywhere. This is not just *your* fight."

And then the eruption of the volcano happened. "I never said that it was, but how dare you question my actions, as a trusted Beta no less! I fought and earned my position." She looked directly at Alak as she yelled. "You think you have any sort of right to reprimand me and in front of a sniveling little man like Dunc?"

Next, she turned her ire on Aeron. "Don't even think about apologizing for him again. He has a mouth and can speak on his own. Clearly, he hasn't mastered the art of holding anything back."

"Why should I hold any of my thoughts back?" Alak roared.

"I only apologize for my brother," Aeron cut in, his own voice rising, "when I know that he regrets his choice of words, because what he has not *mastered* yet, is how to be apologetic or how to put things in a more delicate way. He was not completely off about his meaning, however, with regards to your recent actions."

Katrina took a step back, her mouth open in disbelief. She shook her head and gritted her teeth. "If I was a man, you two chauvinistic pigs would not say this shit to me. My Alpha trusts and respects me. He doesn't question my actions just because I am a female."

Alak was about to speak up. No doubt something he would later regret would tumble out of his mouth, but Aeron put a hand on his chest and spoke to his brother. "I will have my say now. I have held back way too much."

He turned to Katrina. "Your Alpha is not your *mate*," he simply stated. "Alak and I are." He was glad it was finally said aloud amongst the three of them, and even more so that neither one of them dared object, for if either of them had uttered a word to the contrary at that moment, Aeron would have let loose what a volcanic eruption and any other natural disaster would be terrified of. Satisfied, he continued. "This is not about you being a female, and has everything to do with the fact that you are *our* female. We will protect you and care for you without the need for your permission to do so.

"And you are mistaken on quite a few of your suppositions. Alak and I both do respect you. You are a fierce warrior, and had you been a male, mate or not, I would still be concerned for some of your recent actions."

"You don't get to question my actions."

"As I already explained, I absolutely do. You are our mate." He stretched his arm out towards the couch. "Please sit." Her defensive stance did not appear to be letting up, and he much preferred to create a less tense environment for this discussion.

Katrina, however, haughtily arched one of her brows and crossed her arms over her chest.

"I'd like to make it so that she will not be able to sit for a week," Alak grumbled.

Aeron rolled his eyes, obviously, a habit he'd picked up from the frustrating inhabitants of this realm. He chose to ignore Alak's comment rather than apologize for him, especially since his brother's comment was appealing to him as well at the moment.

"Very well, stand if it pleases you," Aeron said before Katrina could speak again. He was not quite finished yet. "You looked puzzled earlier, Katrina, when

Alak paid for the room with that fancy looking card. Gabe had given it to us. Alak simply altered the name."

"O-kay," she said dragging out the word. "What does that have anything to do with what we are discussing right now?"

"Everything," Aeron replied, crossing his arms as well. He was getting more infuriated with her stubbornness by the minute. "I have come to understand the way your currency works here and the greed some have over it. Though Alak and I don't always see eye to eye with your Alphas, I respect them both. They are good leaders, brave warriors, and fierce protectors over their people. They are not wealthy because they are greedy for riches. They use their money to house and protect their pack and pard, to create healing centers for your kind, and even to fund missions such as ours. That vile woman downstairs sought to make you feel less than because you were not able to purchase this room. Neither Alak nor I could allow that."

Alak dipped his head in acknowledgement.

"She wouldn't have succeeded," Katrina said.

"That," Aeron began, "is my point exactly, Katrina. You would be just as happy out in nature if not more so than being here." He made a gesture with his hand indicating the room. "You are worthy of everything we can possibly give you in this world. I just pray that one day you will see that for yourself."

She dropped her hands to her sides, relaxing her pose, but Aeron could clearly see that her emotional guard was still up like a fortress. She stayed silent though, adding to his ire.

"I would also question why you feel the need to get beaten up in that bar for such a small amount of reward, when we have just established that money is clearly not your motivation." Softly, he added, "Male or female does not matter. The reasons behind why you would want to put yourself through all of that does."

Still she said nothing, and Aeron's patience finally snapped. With his voice rising, he said, "You may be a dominant cougar, but make no mistake, little kitten, my brother and I do not take orders."

He took a step toward her, and with her eyes widening, she took a step back.

Another step forward from Aeron, followed by another step back by Katrina. "We will complete our mission together—the three of us—and if you flee, we will follow you."

Their slow forward and backward dance continued until Katrina's back hit the wall and Aeron stood right in front of her, so close in fact that their noses were almost touching. He trapped her with his arms outstretched and against the wall on either side of her head and inhaled her sweet and musky scent, nostrils flaring. "My kind does not have as keen sense of smell as a shifter, but I can still smell your desire, and your very essence is ingrained in me. There will be no place in any realm that you could hide from me."

Katrina swallowed loudly. He might be getting his point across, but that did little to ease the frustrated emotions that flowed through him in this moment.

"And no one," he continued, "will dare hurt you again. Not as long as Alak and I draw breath. You are our mate. It is our right and our privilege to keep you safe. You must accept what that means."

Aeron didn't give her a chance this time to respond or to not respond. Instead, he fused his lips with hers and tasted his mate for the first time, their tongues feverishly entwining. All too soon, he ended their kiss, reluctantly pushing himself away from the wall. This time it was Aeron who took a few steps back.

His heart beat rapidly as he stood there with his gaze locked on hers. He wanted to throw her on the bed and strip her before he fucked her into oblivion, but he was still too riled up. A mating fueled by anger would not result in the relationship he longed to have with her. He felt crazed with both need and revenge against all who ever dared harm his mate.

"I need some air," he finally said. "Even though it'll be the stench of the city." He turned on his heel, sparing his brother only a quick glance, and slammed the door shut behind him.

Chapter Ten

Katrina exhaled sharply as the door swung closed behind Aeron. She hadn't even realized she'd been holding her breath. Hell, as soon as Aeron had pressed his mouth to hers she'd been pretty sure she'd lost the ability to breathe at all.

"I hope you're satisfied," Alak said in a sharp tone, and Katrina swung back in his direction. "My brother is known through all the realms of our kingdom as a leader who is not shaken by anything. And yet, through your actions, you have built a frustration within him I have never felt before, and with the power we both have it would be wise for you to not allow that to happen again, and do as we ask."

Katrina went from dazed and aroused, to pissed as hell in less than a second. The fact that her arousal didn't ebb in the slightest as her rage soared, angered her even more. "*Do as you ask?* Really? You expect a mate to simply accept what you have to say as law and go with it? *Please*, Alak, the fifties called, and they want their stereotypically sexist opinions back."

Alak frowned. "Who is this 'fifties', and why would they call to speak about me?"

Katrina threw her hands in the air, moving away from the wall and further into the hotel room. "You are all powerful and can open a portal between two countries, two realms, and into fucking Narnia for all I know, so why the hell can you not speak sarcasm?"

Alak arched a perfect brow in her direction, and it was all she could do not to reach out, shift her hand into claws, and cut the perfectly shaped arc from his face. "I know what you speak of. Sarcasm is the use of tone or irony that one might use to convey contempt or to mock another. I am fluent in more than sixteen languages, and all known Fae dialects beyond the Veil. Sarcasm is most definitely not a language."

"It's all *I* damn well speak," Kat yelled back. "So if you want to understand me at all, then you'd better learn it!"

Alak crossed his arms over his chest, and Kat refused to watch the erotic roll of muscles in his chest and shoulders at the move. "You are being ridiculous. You stand here and demand that Aeron and I treat you as an equal, and yet you are unable to act responsibly with your own safety. Much like a child. If you are to act like a child, why would you then become enraged if we treat you as such?"

Kat growled low, her cat roaring to the surface so quickly it was only her own iron will that left her in her human form. "What the hell are you talking about? You'd better spell this out for me, Alak, or you and I are about to throw down in a very physical way."

Alak's gaze narrowed. "Why do you come all the way to this place so regularly to fight against other shifters? Aeron asked you a pretty straightforward question, which you stubbornly refused to answer. That tells me that perhaps you are not so keen on the answer yourself."

Kat's skin felt tight as her cougar paced within her. "I am Beta in one of North America's largest pards. When Braxas decided to throw in with Gabe and Corrine, and we united with the pack, we became the largest shifter faction that I know of. Honing our combat skills and ensuring we can protect our weaker members is the responsible thing for a senior member of this faction to do."

Alak stepped a little closer. "That all sounds like a perfectly rehearsed and logical answer, Katrina, but it does not make complete sense. The blessed union between Lady Corrine and her mates is very new, yet you have been coming here for years. You said so yourself. So why? I caught glimpses of the fear you had that came with the loss of control from being held captive. I can even understand your desire to try to reclaim it, but I suspect that there is more to it than just that. Why do you feel the need to travel away from those you are supposed to protect to come here to this city and face adversaries like that hideous man we met this afternoon?"

Katrina couldn't remain stationary any longer and began to pace, moving a few steps away from the sofa and back again. She kept her gaze locked on the man in front of her. "I really don't like being interrogated, Alak. Perhaps it's part of this fucking spell I am casting over you and Aeron that you are continually accusing me of."

"Perhaps it is!" Alak said with a raised voice. The two of them were on the verge of really yelling at each other, and damned if Kat wasn't equal parts enraged and aroused by the exchange. "But this has nothing to do with the fact that you are our mate, we—"

"*Supposedly* your mate," Kat yelled back, throwing her arms in the air in frustration. "Just because you can bring yourself to admit that you have a connection with a lowly shifter doesn't mean that it's real."

Alak growled, his tattoos now flickering into full view. "Of course it is real! Perhaps, I too, feared the connection at first, but a mate is a most cherished gift from the Goddess, one Aeron and I would never forsake. And what is this business about being a lowly shifter? We do not place ourselves above others, and I find it insulting that you would think so."

Kat paced forward a couple of steps. "Yet you can

insult me quite easily! If I *am* your mate then I have to know my place, right?"

"That is not how it would be," Alak all but roared. "But we will never get there if you cannot be honest with me. You cannot even be honest with yourself. Answer the question, Katrina. Why is it that you come here to this place, determined to put yourself in danger, fight these men who could never be worthy of your attention or the right to put their hands on you? Why, Katrina, why?"

"Because I was looking for a mate!" Kat found herself screaming back. "I am a dominant *female* cougar, Alak, and that is rarer than you know. Fucking Beta to a pard, a position I have earned through blood in the way of my kind. There is no male more dominant in our pard than me, except Braxas, and we were not destined for each other. Do you know what it is like to believe that you have been forsaken by the Fates? To believe that there would be no happily ever after for me? Even though I was born dominant, I'm still a woman who longs to be loved, to be held, to be cherished. I see it all around me, and I wanted it for myself. I figured if I came here and fought that I might actually lose. Then perhaps I could find a man more dominant than I, and if that happened I could find my happy ending!"

The only sound in the room for a moment was Katrina's breathing. Alak stood, his arms now by his sides, those lickable tattoos permanently on display, and the expression on his face was hard to read. The desire in his eyes however, was very discernible. Heat pooled within her.

Later, Kat would never be able to say who moved first, but they both crossed the room toward each other. As she reached him, she threw her arms over his shoulders and reveled in the feeling of his muscular arms wrapping around her waist. He pulled her up against his hard chest, and she wrapped her legs around his hips. Alak kept moving, the hard evidence of his arousal pushing against her in the most delicious way. His mouth came down on hers just as he slammed them both into the wall behind her, taking the brunt of the impact with the hand that came up beside her head, and Kat gave herself over to the kiss.

****

Aeron took another calming breath. Never before had he allowed his feelings to overwhelm him to the point where he walked away from a conversation. He always kept a cool head, but Katrina's emotional wall she'd placed between them had shattered that ability. He had only walked to the end of the corridor and was currently pacing back and forth in front of the bank of elevators. Even with the emotions rolling within him, he couldn't bring himself to go too far away from his mate. Despite only having known her for a short while, he was completely drawn to her, and the thought of distance between them had an actual pain forming in his chest.

He reached up to press the palm of his right hand against the ache. He had always imagined that finding his mate would have brought nothing but happiness and joy for the future. This pain and angst were unexpected. Images of his beautiful mate flickered through his mind. The way she looked that first moment he laid eyes on her, despite being covered with blood and fresh from battle, she was a beacon of fierce beauty that called to him like no other. He adored the flash of spirit that flickered through her golden eyes in the moments before she threw her words at him and his brother like sharpened weapons. Their mate was strong, powerful enough to stand toe to toe with the High Dorum and protect those around her with a grace and fierceness he had rarely seen in others.

She was worth the pain and angst they'd face in order to find their way together. She was worth … everything. Filled with a determination to make her see that he and Alak were her future as she was most definitely theirs, he moved quickly back down the hallway toward the room they shared. As he approached the door he could feel the swell of emotion and power in the air. He could also hear raised voices in the room as he reached out to open the door.

"Yet you can insult me quite easily!" Aeron froze at the hurt and accusation in Kat's tone.

"If I *am* your mate then I have to know my place, right?"

He'd thought that perhaps Alak's words and the fact he had allowed Alak to speak that way to their mate might have angered her, but to hear the pain in her voice had his own heart breaking.

"That is not how it would be," Alak yelled back, and Aeron could hear that he, too, hurt for their mate, but as usual, the tone he used told a completely different story. "But we will never get there if you cannot be honest with me. You cannot even be honest with yourself." His brother prompted her for an answer, and Aeron heard a tiny crack of desperation in his voice, one he was sure no one else could have picked up on. "Why, Katrina why?"

Aeron held his breath. Would Katrina find the strength to answer?

"Because I was looking for a mate!" she yelled back, and Aeron closed his eyes, leaning his forehead against the door. He had suspected there was a more personal reason than the financial, more than her need for control, but he had never suspected that.

"I am a dominant *female* cougar, Alak, and that is rarer than you know. Fucking Beta to a pard, a position I have earned through blood in the way of my kind. There is no male more dominant in our pard than me, except Braxas, and we were not destined for each other. Do you know what it is like to believe that you have been forsaken by the Fates? To believe that there would be no happily ever after for me? Even though I was born dominant, I'm still a woman who longs to be loved, to be held, to be cherished. I see it all around me, and I wanted it for myself. I figured if I came here and fought, that I might actually lose, then perhaps I could find a man more dominant than I, and if that happened I could find my happy ending!"

Everything within him cried out that he and Alak were her mates. They were the ones who would be there to love her, to hold her, and to cherish her for as long as they lived.

A light thud came from inside the room that had him lifting his head from the door in shock. Not bothering with the plastic card they had been given that seemed to unlock the door, Aeron used his powers to open the lock, twisted the handle and entered the room. He had no idea what he would find, but he certainly hadn't expected to find his mate and his brother locked in intense embrace against the far wall. Arousal flooded his system.

Alak might struggle to put his emotions into words, but apparently his actions were much easier to interpret. This was their chance to show Katrina that she was destined to be their third, just as he and Alak were fated to be her mates. A slow smile formed as he allowed his glamor to fade, and he moved toward them. He was looking forward to showing their dominant little kitten

that he and Alak were more than worthy of her
submission.

Chapter Eleven

The taste of Katrina on Alak's tongue seemed to only push his control further out of his reach. Her flavor reminded him of the woods near his village. She tasted like home to him. In his rational mind, he knew the fact he had her pinned to the wall with his body, her moaning as he used everything he had to bring her the pleasure they both sought, was only a short reprieve from their dominance battle. However, given how their fierce mate was reacting to his aggression, it appeared that perhaps his and Aeron's plan to give her space to get used to them was poorly chosen. If Katrina was looking for dominant males to rival her own strength, then they should have begun as they intended to carry on. He wouldn't make that mistake again. Although, given his current state— being driven wild with desire by what she was doing right now with her lips—he may be willing to negotiate for.

Sweet Goddess, our mate could drive me mad with her mouth alone…

Katrina released the suction she'd had on his tongue, and Alak groaned as he imagined that action much lower on his body. His cock pulsed in anticipation, and she must have felt it against her own sensitive flesh. She also moaned and ground her hot mound against his shaft still trapped within his clothing.

"Take this off," she said right before she tore at the buttons on his shirt, her legs still wrapped tightly around his hips. "And drop your glamor. I want to see the real you."

Her request threw him for a moment. He thought perhaps she had preferred him and Alak to look more like the men she was used to, but then again, everything she did surprised him. He let the magic fade from his appearance. The lust in her eyes only grew hotter as she took in the breadth of his chest once his shirt was discarded on the floor.

Alak sensed his brother had returned, and he smiled as he grabbed Katrina firmly under her ass and turned her back towards the door, where Aeron was now ridding himself of his own shirt. Katrina closed her eyes and then smiled as she inhaled deeply.

"I can scent you, Aeron," she whispered. "You smell like the night sky right before a thunderstorm. I've always loved to watch the storms."

"And you, love," Aeron groaned as he settled his chest against her back, "smell like home to me. But you are wearing entirely too many clothes for what we all need right now."

Kat bit her bottom lip and nodded in agreement. With one pass of Aeron's magic over her clothing, the seams melted away, and he gently dropped the scraps to the ground, leaving Alak's arms full of warm, golden, naked skin. Alak placed a kiss along her shoulder, up to her neck, while Aeron did the same on the other side. Their mate's arousal was all that was important right now, and Alak could think of nothing else but ensuring her pleasure.

"Just so you both know ... our argument isn't over," she said, her words coming out in short pants in between kisses Aeron and Alak were delivering.

"I'd expect nothing less from our delectable dragon," Alak teased back.

"Are you mocking me?"

Alak saw the tiny smirk at the corner of her mouth, and he pulled her chin towards his own lips before looking straight into her golden eyes. "Never," he said, and then he kissed her with everything he had building up inside of him. His passion, his frustration, his longing, and finally, with all the loneliness he and his brother had endured over their long lifetime. To be High Dorum was the greatest honor the Goddess could bestow upon her children, but it set them apart from the rest of their people. They'd almost lost hope for a mate of their own, for how would one female hold the strength to equal theirs? But the Goddess sees all her children, and she must have known that this remarkable woman was just out there, waiting for Aeron and Alak to follow the path that led to her. Now it was up to them not to screw it up.

"Do you want us, Katrina?" Alak finally pulled back from her lips and whispered his question, as if afraid in this moment that she would deny them all what they so desperately needed.

"I do," she replied without a single hint of hesitation in her voice.

Alak carried her to the master bedroom in their suite with Aeron following closely behind. When they reached the king-sized bed, Katrina lowered herself down the length of him and then positioned herself on her back in the center of the bed. A golden goddess, holding him in place as he gazed upon her in fascination. She stretched out her arms and beckoned them to join her. Finally, he snapped out of his daze, and he and Aeron continued undressing. He loved the little hitch in her breath as they revealed themselves to her, her gaze roaming over their bodies, seemingly greedy to take them in. Alak ached for her. He grabbed his length and slowly stroked, and the sight of her little pink tongue darting out to wet her perfect lips made him groan out her name.

"Katrina, are you wet for us, mate?"

"Yes, do you want to see?" she purred, legs

falling gracefully to each side.

"You make my mouth water seeing you ready for us," Aeron said, his voice strained with desire. "I've thought of this moment many times since we met."

Alak knew all too well what his brother was feeling in this moment—the same kernel of hope was beginning to burn bright in his own heart, that this glorious woman would make their lives complete. He followed Aeron onto the bed and stretched out beside Katrina while Aeron knelt by her feet, his hand slowly stroking along her calf.

"I think it's time we quenched our thirst, brother," Aeron said.

Alak wound his fingers through Katrina's thick golden waves and brought her mouth up to meet his own. He knew when she suddenly sucked in a breath that Aeron had also found his target much lower, and Alak thoroughly enjoyed caressing every inch of her mouth as she chased her pleasure. When Katrina's clever hands moved over his chest and down his stomach, he wasn't certain that he wouldn't embarrass himself once she reached her intended destination. The heat of her touch as she wrapped her hand around his swollen flesh was more intense than he had imagined it—and he *had* imagined this very scene, many times.

"Goddess, Katrina, you undo me," he groaned into her mouth as she explored every inch of his cock with her questing fingers.

"If I make you feel a fraction of the emotions that I get running through me when either of you are near," she panted in between kisses, "then I can almost forgive your boorish behavior since we met."

Alak's brain was quickly losing the ability to banter as her strokes became faster and his hips began to buck into her hold. "You haven't exactly been the picture of feminine restraint, my *dragon*."

The smile that blossomed across her face at his teasing was the most beautiful sight he'd ever seen.

"Yeah," she said with laughter in her voice right before she threw him a wink. "I get that a lot. Now are you going to talk all night, or are you going to bring this big cock up here and give me something better to do with my mouth?"

Her laughter abruptly turned into a moan of pleasure, her body bucking under Aeron's tongue, and Alak didn't have to be told twice. He moved himself further up the bed until his hips were next to Kat's head, and when he ran his fingers along her cheek, her golden eyes snapped open and she licked her full, sensuous lips.

"Mmm, come here, baby."

The entire universe slipped away from him until all that was left was the exhilarating pleasure as soon as her lips wrapped around him and his length disappeared into her mouth.

Chapter Twelve

Katrina's taste on Aeron's tongue was better than the sweetest ambrosia. He slipped two fingers into her needy, wet channel as he sucked down hard on her clit. He pressed down gently on her flat stomach with his free hand to steady her wildly bucking hips as he pulled her orgasm from her, and then he gave her pussy one final kiss before sitting up. The sight before him made him almost impossibly harder.

His mate's face was flushed and more relaxed than he had ever seen, but it was the vision of her sucking on his brother's cock, her plump limps around his shaft, and then her tongue darting out to lick the swollen head that him biting down on his lip. This was a woman who clearly enjoyed giving pleasure as much as she enjoyed receiving it, and he couldn't wait to have those lips wrapped around his own dick.

Right now, though, he needed her, to be inside her, finally laying claim to his mate and sealing their bond. Aeron crawled up her body, trailing kisses along the way, stopping at her breasts to kiss them in turn. When he reached her neck, he positioned himself at her entrance and slowly plunged inside. Just then, Alak let out a loud roar and shouted out their mate's name in reverence, as if calling to a goddess. Katrina, meanwhile, kept her lips around him until she swallowed everything Alak had to give her.

Only when she popped Alak out of her mouth, did Aeron briefly break their connection. He flipped her over on her stomach and pulled her up on all fours. "I can't be gentle now," he told her, his voice husky, just before plunging back inside her.

"I don't want gentle," she replied on a harsh, raspy breath.

That was all the fuel he needed to grab onto her hips, and thrust faster, deeper than he had before in their missionary position. "You feel amazing, my mate." No other prior experience had ever felt this good, nothing he could even remotely compare it to.

He briefly glanced over at his brother to see him staring at Katrina in rapt attention. Alak's cock was hardening again. Aeron wished he could see her face at that moment, but there was no way he could possibly break their connection now. He was too close to coming, and based on how tightly her inner walls were squeezing him, as well as her loud successive moans, his little kitten wasn't far off from her pleasure either.

"Aeron," she called out to him. Her breathing was harsh as she took everything he gave her and pushed back into him to give just as good. "Oh, Goddess, I'm going to come so fucking hard now. I love the way you feel."

"*Ut tu moarre ebe-et,*" Aeron cried out in his native tongue. *As do you, my forever love.*

"You'll have to translate that for me," Katrina said, panting in between words. "It sounds so hot."

Aeron leaned in closer to her, still pounding hard into her. He put his chest flush against her back, while he rubbed her clit with one hand and balanced himself on the other. He whispered the translation in her ear right before he commanded her to come for him.

She did—screaming as she came. He pulled her up in a seated position, their bodies still flush and connected, and wrapped his arms tightly around her as he, too, released inside of her. They rode out the remnants of their orgasm together that way.

What Fae and shifter-kind had most in common was their insatiable need to claim their mate, particularly after their first joining. Aeron felt the tingling in his gums, and his canines elongated slightly and into sharper points. It startled him even though he was expecting it. Unlike shifters, Fae, both light and dark, did not experience these primal animalistic changes except in the case of mating. He heard Katrina let out a low growl, causing his cock to harden and twitch inside of her, and he could wait no longer. The need to mark her became almost painful.

He bit down on her neck, tasting her coppery tang as it flowed from her. It was delicious. Katrina moaned, called out Aeron's name, and then took his wrist and bit down hard on the inside of it. He felt his own blood being pulled, once again surprising him with how extremely pleasant the sensation was, so much so that he began to thrust his hips up into her just as their bond snapped into place, like two parts of a puzzle fitting perfectly together. All that remained absent was the final piece.

They came again in unison, long hard spasms shaking both their bodies. Aeron licked the bite mark he had given her, and then Katrina did the same to the one she bestowed upon him. He spared one more moment to hold her, but no more, knowing that his brother's need had to be met now as well. After a final kiss to her temple, and these whispered words, "*Et me xsorum uskue en aeternum tebi fovum*," he released her to Alak.

****

"Oh Gods, I love your language," Katrina groaned as Alak took her in his arms. She loved the way both men rolled their Rs when they spoke the primary Dark Fae language and how most of the sounds sounded lyrical, melodious, emanating from two slightly varying deep male voices, smooth like velvet most of the time, and gritty, rising an octave when impassioned or angered.

The pair of them continually ignited her, making her feel wild and willing to give up her control. After three earth-shattering orgasms, Katrina wanted more. She would not be sated until she had Alak, too.

He was surprisingly gentle as he kissed her, delivering long slow strokes with his tongue and gentle nips with his teeth against her lips, and then he slid in between her legs and without preamble, thrust inside her.

It soon became apparent that they were on the same page. As sweet as gentle was, and she was certain there may be occasions in the future that called for it, this was not one of them. She wanted raw and dirty, to come just as hard for him as she did for his brother. Taking the cue, Alak sat up and brought her legs up and together over one shoulder, pulling her closer to him and slightly angling her hip in the process. She made an incoherent sound as his thick, long cock slid deeper into her. As he thrust hard and deep, she felt tingling sensations throughout every nerve in her body, causing her to arch her back and throw her hands above her to grip her pillow. The bed shook, and the headboard banged against the wall with the force of his movements.

The room filled with the sounds of Katrina's loud moans and string of curses along with Alak's guttural grunts mixed with musical words. He could have been cursing as well for all she knew, but it all sounded beautiful. Knowing that Aeron was watching them turned her on even more. She felt her orgasm fast approaching like a tidal wave about to bury her in ecstasy.

She gripped the pillow harder as spasm after spasm finally crashed upon her, taking Alak with her. A low, throaty growl built in her throat as her canines dropped. She and her cougar longed to claim their mate, even more so when she saw the feral look on Alak's face, his own teeth now sharp points.

She reached for him, beckoning him to give her what they both wanted. He spread her legs and leaned down over her and then he bit her on the other side of her neck just as she bit down on his wrist. She immediately felt their bond snap into place, even stronger now that their triad was finally complete. Despite being perfectly spent now, the euphoric feeling their blood exchange produced, brought about another intense orgasm, and only then did she finally feel sated.

She couldn't help but smile when Alak looked at her tenderly. She had never seen his normally stern features so soft. *"Et me xsorum uskue en aeternum tebi fovum,"* he whispered to her. They were the same words Aeron had said to her.

Whatever argument she had with the pair of them and them with her, would have to wait until the morning. Not only was she exhausted from the plethora of orgasms and the intensity of the bond she was feeling, she wanted to just relax in post-coital bliss. She was suddenly tired of fighting with them, and of denying the feelings she'd had for them since the moment they first met.

Aeron and Alak snuggled her in between them under the covers, and Katrina had to close her eyes and savor the two heady male scents, a mixture of sex, sweetness, and the smell of a forest after a heavy rain.

She felt herself drifting into what would probably turn out to be one of the most peaceful nights of sleep she had ever had, but their endearing sounding words replayed in her mind and she had to know the meaning.

"What was it that the two of you said after you bit me?" she asked them.

"My mate, I will cherish you forever," Aeron replied.

"Who knew you guys were such romantics," she

said, amusement in her voice.

"There is much you don't know about us yet, dragon," Alak said.

Katrina chuckled at his playful tone, and she looked forward to discovering everything she was ignorant of about her mates even if that discovery entailed more sparring with them. Actually, she looked forward to that, too.

****

Alak couldn't sleep. He'd never before had the tumultuous mixture of emotions that were currently overwhelming him as he watched their mate slumber, content and sated, in between them. *What* exactly was he feeling? Well, there was relief, that Katrina had finally given into the connection between them. Possessiveness, as they now had the most desirable female he'd ever laid eyes on for their fated mate. Pity, for any male who will try to lay claim to her again. Sheer joy, as he imagined what their future might hold for them. And then stark fear, as only the Goddess knew, Alak had never before had so much to lose as he did right in this moment.

"I can *almost* hear you thinking, brother." Aeron's quiet voice interrupted the chaos swirling in Alak's mind. "It's all quite overwhelming, isn't it? The connection and the emotions that come with it."

"It is," he answered, relieved that as always, he had his brother there to navigate this new adventure alongside him. "Part of me just wants to put our mate some place safe to keep her from any and all threats, but the rational part knows that she would string us up if we ever even suggested it." A quiet laugh fell from his lips. "It appears I *can* be trained after all. Won't our little kitten be pleased with herself?"

The answering smile on his brother's face was

filled with a joy he'd not seen in Aeron since they were children, and it warmed his own heart to see it.

"We will keep her safe, brother," Aeron stated simply, and with absolute confidence. "Together, we will keep her safe and serve our Goddess both. Now try to get some rest."

Aeron and Alak had always known from a young age that they were destined to speak for the Goddess and serve her in all things. Their lives had always been so driven, their path so clear. But this new danger ahead, these dark abominations who were selling their dangerous wares to unscrupulous souls, this was uncharted territory for them. They were in unfamiliar surroundings, on a likely very dangerous mission, with the most precious gift they'd ever been given. The three of them needed to be as one cohesive unit, not battling amongst each other, and he vowed to himself that he would try his best to see his beautiful mate's point of view from now on before losing his temper.

Well … most of the time anyway, he thought as a smile broke across his face and he remembered the explosive start to their evening. There certainly was something to be said for arguing with their feisty mate. The expression he'd overheard Corrine and April giggling about in the kitchen one day, suddenly came to mind—make-up sex was the hottest sex. He certainly understood what they meant by that now.

Chapter Thirteen

"What in the name of our righteous Goddess is that smell?"

Katrina grinned at the tone in Alak's voice. Equal parts horror and disgust and she couldn't blame him. "That would be our destination." Kat laughed when both her men grimaced with distaste.

The three of them had roused early this morning, and Kat couldn't help the shiver of pleasure that rolled through her at how they had started the day. Her men had reached for her, as hungry for another taste of her as she was for them. It had taken an impressive amount of willpower from all three of them to actually get up out of the bed and prepare for the day.

They were heading for the heart of the hyena clan, and Kat was determined that by the end of the day, she would have had a conversation with Melanie that would have them a little closer to finding Nyx and Zayden, not to mention figuring out what the hell was going on with this black magic market selling Underfae weaponry.

"Do these creatures have no sense of smell?" Aeron spoke with a slight lisp as if he were forcing himself to breathe only through his mouth.

Katrina turned the last corner, leading the three of them deeper into the convoluted alleyways in a highly industrial area of Detroit. The path would eventually bring them to the hyena clan's den.

"Much like their natural counterparts, shifter hyenas prefer to live in dens with multiple entries and exits," Katrina said as she continued to sweep her gaze over the surrounding rooftops, knowing that there would be sentries posted at all access points. Her men—*her men!*—might be doing their Dark Fae thing and hiding their approach from anyone looking in their direction, but old habits were hard to stop. "It makes it hard for them to be attacked, and would involve whoever came at them spreading their own resources thin to cover them all."

"That all makes sense, my mate, but why does it smell like a *khëndran* has died here three weeks ago and left to rot in the sun?"

Kat laughed at the colorful yet accurate picture Alak painted. "Of all the shifters in this world, hyenas tend to live much like their wild relatives do. In this case, they mark their territories by depositing a very strong-smelling substance produced in their anal glands around the area. It not only marks it as their boundary, but it messes with every other animal's sense of smell, making it damn near impossible to determine how many of them might be in the den at any one time." Katrina had dropped her voice, not wanting to give them away.

"You can speak freely, mate," Aeron said with a small smile, and Kat wondered if he enjoyed calling her that as much as she enjoyed hearing it. "I have shielded us completely from the outside world. No one in this den will know that we are there until such time as you wish it to be so."

Katrina sighed. Her mates were such badasses. The three continued into the den, walking past two women and one man posted at the entrance, all of them on high alert, but having no clue that they'd just walked casually past them and into the heart of their home. The smell and atmosphere changed completely once they were inside the complex—clean, with the hint of something baking in the air, and they heard the sound of children playing nearby.

"They all live together in this den," Kat said in a voice still lowered despite Aeron's assurances. "All who swear fealty to the dominant female will live with her protection within these walls. So different from my pard."

"How so?" Alak queried as they continued further into the den.

"Cougars are a solitary breed. We guard our independence fiercely, but mess with one of us and you'll get the whole damn lot of us prepared to bury our foot up your ass."

Alak and Aeron both laughed at the colorful picture she painted, but it was nothing but the truth. Solitary her pard might be, but they were fiercely protective of one another. They rounded the corner of a long hallway and entered into what appeared to be a large central meeting space. The area was circular with seating that curved right around the room and dropped down into a central well. There had to be at least fifteen levels of seating, with six separate aisles that led down to the bottom of the room where a large dais sat.

There were currently a handful of adult shifters all standing down on the dais talking about training plans from what Kat could tell. Despite the fact that there were females and males in the group, some of whom were huge and simply screamed dominance, there was only one that held the aura of an Alpha. The female at the center of it all had to be Melanie. Katrina saw her entire being freeze as if alerted to something. When the Alpha made a suddenly guttural noise deep, the others all spun outwards looking for whatever danger she had sensed. Two of the larger males ran up the closest stairs, no doubt to warn the others, and lock down the children in the den.

"Interesting," Aeron remarked as he watched the action intently. "The Alpha must have a thread of psychic ability for her to sense that we might be near. It is strong enough that she has a natural shield that makes it impossible for me to read her mind."

Kat sent him a pointed look. "You mean to tell me, all high and mighty Dorum, that a *hyena* shifter is able to sense your Dark Fae magic and block it? Perhaps you are not as all powerful and dominant as you say you are."

Aeron shot her a quick hot grin. "Oh, mate, so you need another lesson on just how powerful and dominant I am? Once we are out of this den with the information we need, I will be only too willing to reeducate you."

Alak reached out to wrap his hand in her ponytail and pulled her hair back, making her moan as sparks of heat and desire burst within her. "And that will go double for me."

Katrina purred, letting both of them know that she was more than open to that idea. When they both stepped closer to her, she could sense their heightened arousal down the newly formed bond between them, and knew she was very close to being fucked in a super-secret psychic bubble in the middle of a hyena den. She'd always thought she might like a little danger of getting caught spice added to her sex life, but now was not the time.

"Not now," Kat said in a voice filled with promise and sin. "Let's get this conversation over with first, and then we can get right on that."

Both men gave her hot looks that clearly said they would be holding her to that promise. Alak released her hair, and the three of them stepped closer to the dais.

"How would you like to proceed, Katrina?"

She jolted in surprise at Alak's question. That was the first time he had ever deferred their next move to her, and she found that just as arousing as when he pulled her hair.

"Are you able to hold the rest of these shifters immobile and block anyone else coming into the area while I have a conversation with Melanie?" Kat asked, a plan forming quickly.

"Yes," both men answered, and Kat got the feeling the request would not cost them much.

"Okay then, you guys do your mind meld thing, and I'll see if I can't get Melanie to share a little information with the rest of the class." Kat turned and winked at her men over her shoulder. "I have a certain way with people."

She left off the part where it usually took a beating or perhaps some explicit and detailed threatening, but she always managed to get the information she was looking for. After all, despite being mated, a woman loved to have an air of mystery about her.

Chapter Fourteen

Alak knew by now that whenever his mate said she wanted to *talk* to someone that things usually ended up bloody. What he couldn't for the life of him explain was why he found that particular trait rather charming about her. Katrina was such a delicious bundle of contradictions. She was absolutely stunning to look at, a true picture of feminine beauty, but Goddess help anyone who treated her like a delicate flower. She had the mouth and attitude to rival any hardened warrior he'd ever met.

He didn't know what to expect from the hyena matriarch. These hyena shifters seemed very different from the wolves, cougars, and bears he'd met so far, and he didn't trust them one bit. Alak concentrated on the barrier they would need, whispering a spell that had the other hyenas distancing themselves from the female before he merged his magic with Aeron's and the barrier was complete, locking Melanie alone inside with them. He was impressed that her senses picked up on their presence at all since most beings didn't feel Fae magic until it was already too late.

"What is going on?" the female barked out as she frantically looked around to her people, who were now all staring blankly into space, frozen for the time being.

"We're just here to talk, Melanie." Katrina stepped forward with her hands raised, revealing herself, and Alak followed suit behind her, not trusting the woman's reaction.

If she was shocked, he couldn't tell. Melanie's eyes only narrowed in suspicion towards Katrina, but when she saw Aeron and Alak, she hissed, sharp claws extending from her finger tips. "I know what you are, Dark Ones. How *dare* you bring these beings into my den."

"You have seen our kind before then?" Aeron asked.

"I've seen more than I ever wanted to, and the memories will haunt me until I die," she answered before turning back to Katrina. "What do you want, feline? The cougars have no foothold in my city."

"We're here for information only, Melanie. Dunc told me that you had dealt with Zayden and might know where he's getting his weapons from."

Melanie's expression changed then from outright rage to curious and somewhat appraising.

"Ah, I know who you are now, little kitty," she said, her voice raspy, and a little on the masculine side for Alak's taste. "My, my, you are a sneaky bitch, aren't you? I can almost see why my brother is so infatuated with you now. You look like a typical prissy cat, yet you come and fight at the arena for sport. You come onto my territory, bold as you please, using Fae magic like it's going out of style. I hear that you are Beta in your pard, is that correct?"

"I am."

"And who are these males you have with you? Are they your pets?" She paused briefly, and then her lips twitched. "Or are you theirs?"

Alak really didn't care for the way this Melanie was looking at him *or* Katrina at this point. She had a carnal interest in her gaze that did not seem too particular as to where it landed.

"They are my mates, so keep your eyes off my property, bitch," Katrina growled in response.

He could feel Aeron's amusement through their link, and Alak tried to stifle his own pleasure at her fierce defense of their virtue. Their mate was so adorable when she was jealous.

"Feisty, aren't you?"

"You have no idea. Now why don't you tell us about this underground market that Zayden took you to so we can be on our way and out of your hair," Katrina pushed on.

Melanie's bravado evaporated at the mention of Zayden and the mysterious market, which only made Alak more curious. For generations, there had been rumors in their community of what happened to Fae when they reached for power that the Lady Goddess had not granted. To look to the Darkness and to use tainted magic was the ultimate taboo to their people. It was said that when a Fae let the Darkness inside, that it festered like a disease, causing the magic user to devolve into horrific beings. These creatures were known as the Underfae in their folklore, but no Dorum or servant of the Goddess had ever seen one in truth and confirmed their existence. This was no doubt exactly why the Goddess had sent them beyond the Veil in the first place. If these monsters that Melanie was so afraid of were indeed the result of corrupted Fae magic, then it was their responsibility to make certain that this evil was stopped.

"You don't want to go where I've been, cat," Melanie answered quietly. "To be honest, I wish I'd never given that bastard Zayden the time of day when he spoke of an alliance, but when he told me about the powers he'd seen, my curiosity got the better of me."

"We need to stop him," Katrina said, with deadly intent in her voice. "He's insane … but, I think you know that already."

"Oh, yes I know that," Melanie replied, her dry laugh betraying her anxiety, "but I won't drag my people into a war with a maniac like Zayden … and those … *things* he has made bargains with to get weapons. They were horrific. He left two of his own men behind as payment to those monsters. *Sacrifices*, he had said. If I hadn't told him I'd consider his offer, I would have no doubt never made it out of there myself."

"You are fooling yourself if you think by ignoring this you will keep your people safe, Melanie." Katrina's tone softened. "Gabe and Braxas are going to do everything in their power to find Zayden and stop him, but we need to know what we're up against. We need to get to that market. This war, when it starts … there won't be any escaping it, and Zayden won't let you stay out of it. It's time to pick a side, Alpha."

Alak could sense the shifters around them fighting to break free, and he felt the strain to contain them just as much as he was sure Aeron did. He wanted to urge Katrina to talk faster, but he had a feeling Melanie would not appreciate any male interference. They stood in silence for several minutes. He could see the indecision warring behind in Melanie's eyes, and then finally, she nodded.

"Fine, I will tell you what I know, and how to get there, but I won't go near it again, not for anyone." Her last words ended on a whisper. Once again, she schooled her features into her earlier bravado. "The tiger called it the Shadow Market, and the kicker is that it's right in the heart of your Alpha's territory. The entrance is in Stanley Park, but when you pass through the gate, it takes you through some kind of portal. I've never felt anything like it, but I could tell from the scents around me that we were no longer in Vancouver."

"They must have somehow created another Veil portal, one we couldn't sense existed," Aeron murmured.

"Veil?" Melanie's sharp eyes narrowed. "What does that mean?"

"It's the space that separates the Fae realm from

the human realm," Alak explained. "What did you see on the other side?"

"It was very dark, so not much at first. We were in some kind of caves, or tunnels. I can't be sure, but we walked for almost an hour before we came to another doorway, which was guarded by an enormous creature … a cross between a giant and a rhinoceros, and it smelled almost as bad as it looked, like it was rotting from the inside out."

Alak glanced at his brother. Dark creatures deformed and smelling of rotting flesh was definitely a sign that the rumors had not only been true, but were worse than they had feared. The Shadow Market and the Underfae were all very real, and so were their weapons. Even the Goddess herself could not predict the repercussions of this kind of perverted magic. The last thing he wanted to do was to take his mate anywhere near this place, but Alak knew now that they had no choice but to see this evil for themselves. He also knew, even before she opened her mouth to speak, that Katrina wouldn't back down no matter how dire the warning.

"Sounds charming," their mate drawled, unfazed. "Why don't you draw us a map? We're burning daylight here."

Chapter Fifteen

"Let me know when you finally pick a side, Melanie," Katrina said, taking the map from the hyena, crudely drawn on a piece of hotel stationery. The three of them took a few steps back. "Keep the pen," Katrina added with a wink and an incline of her head towards the hotel pen.

Aeron's hold on their private bubble flickered momentarily as he prepared to adjust the spectrum that would evict Melanie. Her pack members began moving again, panic written all over their faces from what they must have presumed was their missing Alpha. Alak made the final push, leaving Melanie outside their protective invisible barrier, once again shielding the trio from view from everyone else. The pack members stepped back in surprise as soon as their matriarch suddenly reappeared to them, and then they glanced back and forth between their leader and the now seemingly empty space. Aeron knew that Melanie could no longer see them, but the woman still stared in their direction as if she still could. The smile on her face was smug.

"She would be a good ally indeed," Aeron said. Anyone who could sense their glamor would be. Notably, he thought, she would be a worthy foe, cunning and powerful, nothing like her sniveling brother, Dunc.

"Let us go." Alak took the lead out of the den the way they came in.

When they got back to their room, they packed and then checked out quickly, but before creating a portal that would take them back to Vancouver, Katrina made a phone call to Braxas to inform her Alpha of what they had learned.

"I'll expect you back here within the hour," Aeron

heard Braxas say through the phone.

"Back?" Katrina raised her brows in surprise. "With all due respect, Alpha, this Shadow Market needs to be checked out ASAP. We need to know what we're up against."

"I agree," Braxas replied. He sounded impatient, but not angry. Aeron knew that he respected and trusted his Beta, but he suspected the Alpha had newly formed concerns from the intel he just received from Katrina. "But I will not send you in again without a solid plan and back-up, Kat."

Katrina opened her mouth to speak, but Braxas continued. "I know you can handle yourself, but I'll not have you going on a suicide mission."

Alak frowned. "Does he not think that we are back-up enough? That we cannot protect our own mate?"

Braxas sighed, his shifter hearing no doubt catching everything Alak had said.

"We will keep her safe," Aeron said. He kept his own annoyance out of his tone. If it had been anyone other than the two Alphas he had come to respect who questioned his mate's safety whilst under his care, he would have had more than a few choice words for them, but he knew that Braxas was simply concerned for his Beta, and most likely even more unnerved than he let on. After all, Katrina and Gabe both had already been victims of the dark magic created by the Underfae. They had both nearly lost their lives.

There was a short pause in the conversation before Braxas spoke again. "Mate, huh? I suppose I'll have to learn to defer to your *mates* sometimes from now on." Another pause. "Please be careful ... all of you," he added quietly before disconnecting the call.

Aeron was actually touched that his concern had included him and his brother, especially now that they would be connected beyond just this mission to stop an evil that threatens both sides of the Veil.

Alak took Katrina's hand. "Never doubt that we will keep you safe, Katrina."

Before their feisty mate could open her mouth to speak, his brother kissed her, passionately, thus leaving her both speechless and breathless, even when they pulled apart. Aeron wasted no time swooping right in and delivering his own breath-stealing kiss, his tongue dueling fiercely with hers as soon as she opened for him. He felt desperate for more of her, all of her, a hunger he was getting used to and no longer reluctant to have, but now was not the time. He also knew that some of this desperation was heightened by the fact that they were about to face an unknown danger. He an Alak would protect her though … with their lives if it came down to that.

Reluctantly, Aeron ended their kiss. "We must go now."

The trip through the portal was far less challenging this time. They no longer needed access to Katrina's mind to get where they needed to go, but she volunteered a part of herself and let them *see*. Aeron saw flashes of their previous night together and this morning. Her euphoria emitted boldly through their link. Warmth squeezed his chest, and he could feel the same sensation echoing in his brother's heart through their bond.

Emotions ran high for all three of them by the time they exited the portal and found themselves right back where they started. Katrina cleared her throat. "Let's leave the bags here. I'll text Braxas so someone from the house can come get them. Can you two pull the park's location from my memories? We could go back to the house and grab a ride, but it'll take about twenty minutes to drive there."

"Of course, the portal will be faster." Alak kissed her gently before laying his palm on her cheek and closing his eyes as Katrina concentrated on the location they would need.

When she finished with the texting, the technology still a bit foreign to him, he opened the portal and the three of them walked hand in hand through it to their destination. As soon as they arrived, a sickening feeling churned in his gut. Katrina drew them away from what she referred to as the main tourist areas and into the woods, and he could feel the dark magic that could only be the entrance they were seeking.

"Um ... hello?"

Katrina's hand waving in front of Aeron's face caught his attention. Apparently, she had been speaking to him while he was distracted by what was beyond the gate. "I'm sorry, love. You were saying something?"

"Yes, I asked—twice actually—if we could be invisible to the outside world again like we were back at the den. What was with you two? It was like you were in a trance or something."

Alak answered. "I don't like this feeling I'm getting."

"Nor do I, brother."

"What do you see up ahead?" Katrina asked. "Is it the entrance to the Veil?"

"It is *an* entrance," Aeron replied. "Not ours though. I think it goes somewhere that should not exist or, rather, no mortal should have access to."

"None of this should exist, Aeron. Not these Underfae or the Shadow Market, or their poisonous, unnatural weapons, but by the Goddess, you don't think..." Alak shook his head.

"What are the two of you not saying in your

super-secret twin code?" Katrina snapped impatiently. "My cougar is frantic, ready to pounce the hell out of here in the other direction."

His mate had good instincts, Aeron thought. Aeron's own horror and disgust warred inside of him, as if begging him to dismiss his theory. "I not only think it, I feel it standing here. That entrance leads to death."

"The Shadow Realm," Alak spat in anger.

"The Shadow Realm?" Katrina tugged on Aeron's arm, urging him to look at her. "That's where Kheelan's poison had sent Gabe's Beta, Donovan, along with his brother, Jason. They nearly didn't make it out of there."

"We were informed of this," Alak said. The three of them stood in a circle now, facing one another. "Donovan and Jason's souls were trapped, while their bodies remained on Earth. No wonder these Underfae are rumored to be deformed. They have found a way to construct a pocket within this realm to create their atrocities, thus not only corrupting their souls, but their bodies as well."

Aeron's heart beat frantically. Earlier, when he thought that they were only going somewhere in the Fae Realm, it felt right to have his mate there with him and Alak, but now... "Katrina—I—we..."

"No," his mate said firmly. "I go where the two of you go. Melanie made it out, and both Zayden and Nyx go back and forth seemingly all the time."

Aeron took Katrina's hand. "Their bodies may not have been corrupted yet, but what of their souls? Perhaps Melanie still remains whole, but do not tell me you do not see the damage in Zayden and Nyx."

Before Katrina could answer, Alak let out a harsh breath and whispered. "It is our fault, brother." Both Aeron and Katrina looked at him. "Frederych! We banished him, but we should have kept a close eye on him. We should have stopped him. We should have made our presence known to the Light Fae sooner and intervened."

Aeron put his free hand on his brother's shoulder while Katrina entwined her other hand with Alak's. *Should haves* would be of no use to them now. "We will do better. We will stop them all this time." Another couple came to mind just then. Rhana and her husband, Lomer. He saw that same self-righteous gleam in their eyes at the council meeting as he had once seen in Frederych. He would make sure that those two would be watched closely so at least that one mistake would never be repeated.

"What are we waiting for?" Katrina asked. "I know you won't let anything happen to me in there. I trust you both with my life." Katrina's face was completely open. Aeron saw fear, but also determination and bravery, and he saw something else, another reason why Braxas had chosen this headstrong woman to be his second—she knew when it was better for a mission to stand down and follow another's lead.

Aeron kissed Katrina, quickly but fervently on the mouth, and Alak followed suit. "We will not be able to be invisible this time," he said answering her earlier question. "The Dark ... the Underfae would no doubt sense our presence. We must assume they have learned to maneuver through the pocket of this Shadow Realm and therefore, will have the advantage, but perhaps a glamor, disguising who we are may let us go unnoticed."

With the glamor in place, the three of them stepped into the portal. Aeron only hoped that they hadn't just sealed their fates into something far worse than death.

Chapter Sixteen

"Something bothering you, mate?"

Kat turned to scowl at Aeron. "I just want to know why the hell is it that when you're in charge of this glamor thing, you both look like sex on legs, and I look like I've been dragged through a bush backwards?"

The three of them had been walking for close to forty minutes through this strange new world, and her frustration had been enough to keep her from falling into a depression she knew would have been spawned from the environment around them. This Shadow Realm was like nothing she had ever experienced before. This world was a cold, barren wasteland with an inexplicable dark light about it. Not day, not true night, just something in between, and when she looked up, she couldn't see one star. In a word it was depressing, and venting her frustrations helped her to keep her mind on the task at hand.

"I should think the reasoning behind that was obvious, my dragon."

The amusement in Alak's tone was the only thing *obvious* to her, and Kat bared her teeth in his direction, which only seemed to amuse him more.

"Not so much, Alak, so why don't you enlighten me?"

Alak's grin had her insides melting and heat pooling low in her abdomen. "It's really quite simple. My brother and I are as possessive as they come, mate of mine. I do not like it when other men look at you with desire in their eyes, and with how stunningly beautiful you are, it is impossible for them not to. If, once we get to this Shadow Market, we encounter any man who dares to look upon you with interest, I would react without thinking. It is difficult to question someone who is no longer breathing, is it not?"

Kat came to an abrupt halt. "Wait. I'm walking around done up like Frankenstein's more unfortunate looking sister because you two don't want other men to look at me?"

Aeron turned with a grin. "Yes, mate. Besides, with what this place does to a person, Dark Fae or otherwise, you do not want to draw attention to yourself. And looking as perfect as you do in your natural form, we are simply looking out for you."

Kat quirked a brow at her mates and started forward once more. Being a mated woman was mellowing her. Rather than ripping them both apart for their overhanded tactics, she found it strangely adorable. She had often wondered what it would be like to have mates of her own, and she was staring to really love how it felt.

Alak's head came up sharply, the movement drawing her out of her contemplation, and immediately on the task at hand. She drew her cougar to the surface, tasting the air around them despite the stench, looking for whatever danger Alak had alerted upon.

"There are more of these Underfae than we anticipated." Alak turned, his eyes swirling with color, another sign of his immense power. "I know it would prove fruitless to ask that you stay behind, mate, so all I will ask is that you allow us to pose the questions?"

Kat narrowed her gaze at him. "This is not my first rodeo, baby, but … I will concede that in this case you and Aeron should take the lead. You know more about this magic mumbo jumbo than me, so that makes sense."

Alak released a long puff of breath as if he had been holding it in anticipation of her answer to their request. "Thank you, dragon."

Kat grinned wickedly back. "Don't get too used to it, mate. It won't happen often."

Aeron stepped closer to her and swept a hand over her ass, causing a shiver to roll through her. "We have no doubt of that, my love."

The three of them continued forward, and Kat had to breathe through her mouth in a desperate attempt not to gag at the stench as they drew nearer to what must be the Shadow Realm market. The sounds of people talking grew louder as they neared the edge of a rocky outcrop they had been following. When they stepped around it, Kat was surprised at the scene that lay before her.

For an underworld market in the middle of an inhospitable environment such as the Shadow Realm, it looked surprisingly homey. The walls of the small barn-like structure were made of the schist type rocks that dotted this strange landscape. The double pitched roof loomed up against the dark sky, and Kat was fairly certain she could see smoke rising from a small chimney. The only thing that seemed out of place was the small size of the building itself.

Aeron muttered something in the strange lyrical language of the Fae, but didn't translate for her so she figured it wasn't anything important.

They neared the path that led to the building when a voice called from somewhere in the gloomy darkness ahead of them, "What business do you have here?"

Kat was a little shocked that these bastards spoke English.

"We have it on good authority that you have a kind of weaponry we are in need of," Aeron called back.

"Is that so?" There was no missing the caution in

the man's tone. He looked to be Dark Fae, and though his outward appearance not wholly grotesque, Kat did not miss the signs of decay running along one side of his neck—cracked skin and blisters, some already ruptured. "What are you looking for, and who told you how to find us?"

Aeron tensed, and Kat frowned as she watched the glamor that hid his true form shimmer briefly before settling back into place.

"We are looking for information about the weapons you sell to the Earth Realm shifters, charged with the force of the Underfae." Kat's frowned deepened at the tone in her mate's voice. Never before had she heard his voice sound so flat. "Invite us forth. You do not need to know who informed us about this market's existence."

There was a moment when the air seemed to thicken. "Come on in, have a look around. We don't need to know who sent you."

Kat turned to Alak. "What the hell is going on? Why does everyone speak English, and that guy is suddenly all trusting?"

Alak grinned. "You are mated to two very powerful Dark Fae, dragon. They are actually *not* speaking English. Aeron has cast a spell that enables you to understand our language, and what you witnessed there was nothing more than a little mind manipulation."

Kat took a moment, as the three of them moved closer to the building, to absorb all of that. "Who freakin' knew that I would be the destined mate for two freakin' Jedi?" She made a sweeping motion in the air with her hand while saying, "These are not the droids you are looking for."

"What is this Jedi?" Alak asked, and it took everything she had not to burst out laughing. She was suddenly hit with how much fun it was going to be to share some of who she was and what it was like to live in the Earth realm with her mates. Not wanting to launch into the joys of the *Star Wars* franchise, Kat shook her head and smiled, making a mental note to plan a movie night once they were safe at home. The George Lucas world would take a little longer to truly bring to life.

When the three of them stepped across the threshold of the small structure, Kat felt more like she was in an episode of *Dr. Who* rather than *Star Wars*. This building might look small from the outside, but once they stepped inside, like the Doctor's beloved Tardis, it opened into a much larger space. There were stalls, for lack of a better word, spread throughout the building selling all manner of otherworldly goods, some of which looked very much like weapons, but also clothing and wares that any good warrior would want. The stench of the outside world had diminished somewhat, but Kat was more shaken by the beings that manned the stalls and those that wondered the aisles.

She knew that the people who paused too long in the Shadow Realm were physically altered by it, but she never imagined how drastic that change would be. These creatures had all once been like her men, proud Dark Fae with a strong heritage and link to their Goddess, but each one of them had tried to corrupt that purity and paid the price for it. These Underfae deserved everything they got as far as she was concerned.

They had determined earlier that they would ascertain the size of the threat in the building before Aeron and Alak brought the market down around them. Kat walked through the space behind Aeron, Alak following her, and tried not to stare at the sights that lay on the display tables before her. When Aeron came to a sudden halt, she almost walked straight into him. Looking over his shoulder she saw two large tables side by side, with strange looking items on them. One had restraints identical to the ones Nyx had used to abduct her. They had cut her off from her cougar, and just looking at them now, she felt the rise of her animal within her, both of them unhappy with the reminder of that time, and what those fucking cuffs represented.

Then her gaze drifted to the other table, and her stomach roiled. There were vials and jars filled with different colored liquids, powders and objects she was fairly certain were teeth. Whatever the spell Aeron had cast upon her, it enabled her to read the labels. There was ground bone from both humans and various shifters, the venom of snake shifters, the ground liver of tiger shifters. Each was more horrendous than the last. Kat's heart stuttered in her chest when she saw the label on one of those jars clearly read "Cougar Teeth".

Horror and anger warred for supremacy within her, and her cougar pushed to the fore. Alak suddenly reached out and grabbed her hand. Kat felt a pulse of power, not unpleasant or exactly pleasurable, but somehow stopping the spontaneous shift.

"Easy, dragon," Alak murmured. "We will soon burn this abomination to the ground. I promise you, we will make these bastards pay."

Kat stood still, practically vibrating with the need to shift and shred these bastards as fast as possible.

"These items are as forbidden as they are atrocious." Aeron spoke to the stall vendor in that same tone that told Kat he was doing his manipulation thing again. "What gives you the right to trade in such things?"

The vendor frowned, grimacing as if he was in pain, and Kat guessed he must have been fighting whatever Aeron was doing to him. She felt Alak tense beside her, obviously adding more weight to the powerful magic Aeron was using.

"We used to deal with a Dark Fae called Frederych," the man snarled in a voice that came across in a dual tone, as if two people were speaking at the same time. "He shared with us his unique approach on things. We are more powerful than any in the human realm. We trade in whatever we want. Everything you need to increase your own powers, you will find in these markets."

These. There was more than one of these places?

"Aeron," Alak growled. Kat was beginning to understand her mates better now, and a quick glance at Aeron and she could see why Alak had cast his warning. His glamor was slipping, and her handsome mate was coming into view.

"Who are you?" the vendor asked in a wary tone.

Aeron grinned, but there was nothing friendly or warm about it. "I am the one who is going to end this *right* you think you have to free trade. My mate wants this place burnt to the ground." Kat was amazed to see Aeron's tattoos begin to slide from his body, the ink swirling together to form a dark mass of energy that began to move around the room, flame bursting from whatever it touched. "And it is my job to ensure that she gets everything she wants."

Aeron's eyes became completely black, and Kat stepped forward, pressing her hand against his chest. A whimpered sound of fear escaped when she registered that his heart no longer beat.

"It's okay, Katrina," Alak said as he pulled her back against his chest, holding her safe against him. "Aeron has sent his *Akh'Faer* forth to deal with this filth."

"What does that mean?" Kat whispered

"*Akh'Faer* must not have a translation in English, but it is like an army that we wear as adornment. Only the most powerful of our people are blessed in such a way. Each of the lines that mark our bodies has a meaning, and when they come together, they have a strength and a power that is very difficult to stop. Our Goddess gifted us with many talents and skills to protect our people. This is one of the more deadly of those abilities. The downside is, we are completely vulnerable when we do this, which is why when one of us in this form, the other will remain to protect them."

Kat watched as the dark mass Alak referred to as Aeron's warriors swept around the room, lighting everything it touched, the screams of the beasts who worked the market echoing in its wake. Despite the carnage around her, Kat was more than a little in awe of her mate's powers. Knowing that there were more of these places meant that she would get to see her men open up a can of Dark Fae, High Dorum whoop-ass more than once, and she could hardly wait.

Chapter Seventeen

Alak watched their surroundings cautiously as he let his brother take care of the destruction of the Shadow Market. He could already feel the strange pull of this realm's magic, trying to invade and corrupt his body and soul. As Dorum in service to the Goddess, they were more attuned to magic than most of the Fae, and he could understand how some of these poor misled souls would not have realized the cost of their greed until it was too late and there was no longer a place for their twisted existences in the Goddess's realm. It was a fool's errand to reach for power that was not meant to be yours.

The chaos unfolding all around them was overwhelming. Most of the vendors were screaming and fleeing. Only those who tried to save their forbidden contraband were being consumed by Aeron's wrath. They were lucky these Underfae beings weren't organized to defend this place. No doubt the next market they descended upon, the attack would have to be carefully planned once word spread of what they'd done here.

Suddenly, an ear-piercing screech rang out from behind them, and Alak barely had enough time to pull both Kat and Aeron to the ground before an enormous creature came charging onto the scene. It was as grotesque as it was loud, the thick grey skin mottled with sores and open wounds. The beast stood over seven feet tall and had a completely feral look in its eyes as it tried to assess the attack. There was something vaguely familiar about its form, and then it dawned on Alak—this creature must have been one of the forest folk before it had become Underfae.

"Sweet Goddess, what is that stench?" Kat groaned from beside him as she checked on Aeron, who was still unresponsive as his *Akh'Faer* continued its destruction.

"The creature, I believe that this is the one Melanie warned us about. It appears to be decomposing." He watched it carefully for a moment as it swung at the flames, as if it were trying to fight them, but did not know how.

"Sheesh, look at it," Katrina whispered. "I almost feel sorry for him. It's like he's too stupid to know what fire is."

"I can only assume that once the body begins to decompose here that the brain function would fail quickly as well. It makes me wonder how long the Underfae can survive once they begin to devolve."

By now the entirety of the market was going up in smoke and Alak felt his brother's magic begin to return to his body, but he must have used a great deal of energy as it seemed a slower process than normal.

"Looks like this is our cue to take our leave, brother." Alak stood and offered his hand to Katrina, pulling her up when she took it. "Aeron, are you well? The return of your *Akh'Faer* seemed different somehow."

"I think I'm fine—"

"Oh shit." Her face suddenly went pale as she looked over his shoulder. "We have a problem."

Alak and Aeron turned to look at the same time, and though he was sure the beast was less than intelligent, there was no mistaking the anger and hatred etched upon its ugly visage. It stared directly at them for several seconds, then with a roar, it charged forward.

He lashed out with his magic, opening a huge cut right across the creature's chest, sending black blood flying through the air. The grotesque droplets sizzled like acid everywhere they touched. Alak saw Katrina's glamor flicker and then fade as her beast rose higher in response to the attack.

"Katrina, do not shift. Your cougar will not function well here in the Shadow Realm," he yelled out to her as he struck the creature once again. "And don't let the blood get on you either. We don't know how much damage it can do."

"Fine, I can use my fists then, but only if I have to." His mate's frustration was clear in her tone, but Alak didn't want her anywhere near this being regardless.

Aeron must have been exhausted after setting his *Akh'Faer* loose the way he did, but still he charged the creature, ducking under giant arms intent on ripping them limb from limb, slashing out at the beast's knees. But as it fell, one meaty paw connected with Aeron's shoulder, its claws sinking in deep before it tossed him back at Alak, who barely had time to catch his flailing body.

"Aeron!" Katrina screamed as she knelt by his brother's now unconscious form. "We need to leave, Alak!"

The creature was still struggling to stand, but the determination on its face clearly showed that it wasn't caring about its wounds, and Alak had to end this now to get his brother and their mate back to safety. To their left, the still burning structure of a vendor stall caught his eye, and he used everything he had left to pick up the flaming pillars and send them flying through the air until they'd all pierced the giant's body. The scream that left the creature's mouth was horrific, but he did not get back on his feet and Alak wasn't about to stick around to see how quickly he recovered. This beast was so much stronger than it ever should have been.

Alak threw Aeron's prone form over one shoulder and grabbed Katrina's hand in his own before they sprinted back to the portal that had brought them to this cursed place. The journey seemed longer on the way back even though their pace was much quicker and less cautious. That creature had been stronger than he could have imagined, but then again, once a being's logic and reason were destroyed by the invading darkness, only rage and malevolence would be left in its place. They would need a better plan the next time they went hunting for Underfae. Perhaps the Goddess would finally be able to provide them with some insight as to these beings' weaknesses now that they had information to give her. Guns would not work in the Shadow Realm, and if the shifters were to join the battle at their side, it was too dangerous for them to attack with teeth and claws, especially not with the possibility of contamination. By the looks of the festering sores and caustic rotting blood on those creatures, it was unwise to risk themselves until they knew more about their new enemies.

It was dark by the time they exited the portal and entered the woods in the park. Aeron had regained consciousness, but the wounds on his shoulder were concerning.

Katrina pulled back the torn collar of his shift to reveal the dark lines creeping out from the claw marks. "This looks really bad, Aeron. How are you feeling?"

"Like I was skewered and tossed by a giant?" Aeron tried to smile at his mate.

"Now you want to learn how to make jokes?" she asked incredulously. "We need to get you to Erica and April as soon as possible."

"I will open a portal to Gabe's." Aeron was in need of immediate attention. Alak propped his brother up to stand. "Katrina, can you hold him for a moment?"

"I am perfectly capable of standing, thank you." Aeron scowled at him, but Alak could see how unsteady his brother was and it worried him.

There had been very little he and Aeron had feared since the Goddess had blessed them as her High Dorum, but this wild, dark magic was unlike anything they'd faced before. They needed a plan, because he wasn't about to risk those he loved to this malicious infestation. How had such evil been growing right under their noses for all these years? After Aeron was attended to, they would return home to speak to the Goddess Rysanna. Now that they had more information about the Underfae, perhaps the Goddess would know how to go about defeating them.

Chapter Eighteen

Corrine gasped at the sight of Aeron. "Dear Goddess, I never thought I'd see one of you get injured like this."

Despite Aeron's grumblings that he could walk over to the couch on his own, Alak and his mate insisted on providing support and then they sat down on either side of him while they waited for Erica and April to arrive. Gabe, Braxas, and Corrine sat opposite them while a few others in their pack lingered outside the den, fortunately giving them some space. He didn't admit the fact that he actually needed the help, not wanting to worry his brother, and especially Katrina. Corrine had just essentially echoed his own sentiments. Though not immortal, Aeron couldn't think of anything in any realm that could mortally wound him and Alak. These slashes, however, felt different from anything he had ever experienced. Besides the excruciating pain, something seemed to be spreading within him like a poison, eating away at him and blackening his insides.

Corrine's face darkened. "Aeron, I—"

"I know, Lady Corrine," he said solemnly. This poison was akin to the one Corrine had inadvertently brought upon herself when she had tampered with dark magic to save her mate, but even more powerful.

"What?" Katrina glanced between him and Corrine and then at Alak, who no doubt understood their cryptic exchange. "Someone better tell me what the fuck is going on."

Aeron hated the panic he heard in her voice and wished that he could soothe it away, but it was best she prepared herself for the worst. Wordlessly, because he did not think he had strength enough to talk, he took her hand in his, entwining their fingers.

Alak's voice was angry and determined when he answered for him about the poison. "He will live, my mate. I swear it by the Goddess.

Katrina nodded with a look of steely determination written across her face. Aeron wouldn't leave her or Alak. Not without one hell of a fight.

Alak began to brief the others in on their discovery of not only the market they had destroyed, but the location and the fact that there were multiple markets still in existence.

"If any of you should come into contact with the Underfae, try not to draw blood," Alak said. "I do not believe their blood will act as a poison if it does not come in direct contact with broken flesh, but it may burn you." He went on to explain the best approach in fighting them was to tear their limbs and snap their necks. They delivered their poison through teeth and claws, but the more corrupt and poisonous they were, the slower and less intelligent they were as well.

April and her mates arrived on the tail end of the conversation.

"Wait," her mate Donovan warned before she placed her hand on Aeron. "Didn't they just say it was poison?"

Aeron shook his head and gasped as he tried to speak. He heard Katrina's soft whimper at his side, and she squeezed his hand tighter.

"This appears to be the same dark magic that has affected some of you," Alak answered instead once again. "Donovan and Jason's bite, Corrine's use of a dark potion and spell, and the dagger that sliced through Gabe, not to mention the cuffs that were able to suppress shifting and healing, all had properties of the same insidious substance. She has no open wounds for the poison to come in contact with." Alak then quickly filled the trio in on the earlier part of the conversation they had missed to reassure them.

The biggest difference in the toxins had to do with their strength, Aeron surmised. The dark objects, and even the Fae who'd bitten the wolf brothers, had all been infused, whereas in the Underfae, the poison spread like a disease as part of the corruption of the body and soul. He had felt the creature's unnatural decay when the beast had sliced into him.

Donovan still did not look convinced, not that Aeron could blame him, but he gave April a slight, almost imperceptible nod.

She gently placed her hand over his wound and let her healing energy flow. Aeron had to grit his teeth in order to keep from screaming, but then the deafening roar in the room, which he recognized came from him, made him realize he was unsuccessful in his attempt.

"Why isn't it working?" his mate cried. He heard a few other voices ring around the room, but he could not decipher the muffled sounds.

Instead, Aeron closed his eyes and focused on the good energy in his body as well as April's healing one. Another healing force intermingled with hers shortly after, and he realized Erica had joined them. Their combined energy was strong as it battled the darkness inside of him, but all they could do in the end was to mitigate the effects of the poison. They could not obliterate it.

Finally, he managed to stop screaming long enough to tell them to stop. He felt both April and Erica's strength waning from their efforts. "You've done all you could do, and I am grateful. Our Goddess must do the rest."

"Will she be able to heal you, Aeron?" Katrina

asked, her voice panicked.

Aeron nodded and Alak said, "If he can be fully healed, it must be by the Goddess herself. This," he gestured toward Aeron's festering wound, "is beyond what any of our realms have witnessed before. We also must converse with her immediately to let her know about all that has transpired in the Shadow Realm."

What they did not know was who was running the show. It certainly could not be Zayden, or the dim-witted Nyx. They were merely pawns.

No matter, Aeron thought, *I will see them all burned down to the ground, wherever their locations are.*

Alak wasted no time in making a portal from the pack house directly to their own home in the Dark Fae village. Katrina and Alak ignored his protests again and supported him as they made their way through the portal together. Alak had promised Gabe and Braxas to return once Aeron was fully healed and rested and they'd had time to speak with Rysanna to get some answers about all that had transpired. A course of action would need to be plotted, one that required all the help they could get.

"You want me to meet your Goddess?" Katrina asked. Aeron had no idea why she sounded so surprised.

"You are our mate, my love," Aeron wheezed in reply.

"Save your strength, Aeron. Please." She gently cupped his face and delivered a sweet kiss to his forehead.

"Take each of our hands," Alak said to her, and she easily complied. They were sitting in a circle in their garden with Aeron propped against a stone pillar, the top of which contained growing wildflowers from seeds obtained in their lush forest. He could hear the sounds of a nearby waterfall and the rustling of leaves made by a gentle wind. This was where he and Alak by far felt the most peaceful. "There is no one we've ever wanted to introduce to our Goddess more than you, my beautiful dragon, and no one worthier. Close your eyes and concentrate on the vision we will share with you."

Katrina closed her eyes, and then Aeron followed suit. He and Alak, through their bond, focused on Rysanna and the cozy living room she liked to meet in. There was always a roaring fire and two plush adjacent facing couches waiting for them. He and his brother showed this vision to their mate, and within moments, the three of them were seated together opposite their Goddess, her long dark hair braided and draped across one shoulder.

He glanced over at his mate to find her staring in awe at his somber-looking Goddess. Katrina then schooled her features quickly. "Please help my mate, Goddess Rysanna," she pleaded.

He admired his mate's bravado, caring for her mate more than the fact that she was for the first time in her life face to face with a deity. And she was right of course. There would, he hoped, be time later for proper introductions. Right now, his pain still bordered on excruciating.

"Of course, dear one," Rysanna said as she stood from the couch and walked toward them. She knelt in front of Aeron, her eyes wide at the sight of his wound. She closed her eyes and furrowed her brows. Aeron could feel her energy around him, in him, and immediately he understood she was trying to connect with and gauge the properties of the poison within him. It was what he and his brother had done with Corrine's darkness. When Rysanna opened her eyes again, they were wide and fearful, and Aeron felt a sadness sink deep into the pit of his stomach.

"My sister's children did quite well with this wound, but not enough, and I'm afraid even I cannot heal him—"

"No," Katrina shrieked, jumping up from the couch. "He has been loyally serving you for practically his entire life. Do not tell me that a powerful Goddess such as yourself cannot help him."

"It'll be all right, my love," Aeron said, reaching for her hand. When she gave it to him, he gently squeezed, and she took her place beside him again, a heart-wrenching sob escaping her.

"Hush, my child," his Goddess cooed. "You did not let me finish. I cannot heal him *alone*, is what I was about to say." She closed her eyes briefly, and when she opened them again, she said, "All will be well soon." Turning to Alak, she added, "In the meantime, tell me what you've learned. I felt your presence leave the human realm and enter the one of Shadow. Is this not true?"

"You are correct, my lady." Alak filled her in on what transpired in the Shadow Market and all they had learned. All the while his Goddess continued to hold Aeron's hand, lessening his pain in the process.

"What is *that*?" Katrina suddenly asked.

Aeron followed her line of sight and immediately discovered what she was referring to. Granted that part of the room was cast in shadow and all three of them had been preoccupied when they had first arrived, but there was no mistaking what he saw now. A prone figure lay in a fetal position just off to the left of the couch they were currently occupying.

The Goddess sighed, a sad expression on her face. "I heard him call for me among the flames that burned him, but he was less than cooperative. And now I know why he was burning."

"So you killed him?" Katrina asked aghast.

"He was already heading toward death, daughter of the Earth. He managed to give me one bit of information, so I soothed the pain that I could before he met his end. I know that he had chosen a dark path, but he was still one of mine. A mother's love never fades, even if that child turns away from her..."

Among the flames that burned him. "He was one of the Underfae from the market." It wasn't a question. Aeron already knew the answer.

Rysanna nodded anyway. "My children, I have not been completely forthcoming, and I see the folly in that now." She turned away from them and faced the man lying on the floor. "It was truth I spoke when I explained I did not know what this new threat was, but a lie by omission I did not state that, in fact, I had my suspicions. You see, a long time ago, my dear Allyria and I had another sister."

Both he and Alak gasped at this revelation. Their Goddess, who chose and entrusted him and his brother to be the protectors of their people, did not disclose something as important as the existence of another Goddess.

"Please understand I withheld this information not to deceive, but because it was too painful to discuss," she went on, still looking away from them. "Lilliana was the space between light and dark. She was emotion, desire, and the best and worst of both of us. She called the creation of our children burdens and too much responsibility, so she chose not to have any. Though she never seemed to regret her decision, she wanted so desperately to be loved by them. They respected her, yes, but their love was for Allyria and me.

"One day, she fell in love with one of my Dark

Fae children, but as the three of you well know about the existence of mates, he was not hers and he did not return her love. My sister and I watched as she slowly fell into despair, and then madness. They were silly tantrums at first, but then they escalated to something much more sinister. She brought both Fae Realms to their knees with the force of her earthquakes and floods. Many had perished before we had the chance to intervene, for my sister and I did not know the depths she would sink to.

"We meant to capture her, to make her see reason, until we discovered exactly how far she had gone. She killed the mate of the Dark Fae she was infatuated with and turned him into something unnatural and grotesque, enslaving him in the process. She wanted to make him suffer, and to bear witness to her attempts at creating the perfect being, one who would love her eternally. She tampered with our children, both Light and Dark, and she even used the children of Gods and Goddesses of the Earth realm. Somehow, she became stronger and more powerful by creating her own type of dark magic and ingesting it. The *things* she had created," Aeron heard the disgust in her tone, "they were too twisted up inside to be capable of such an emotion as love, but they worshipped and followed her, and all the while their outwardly appearance, as well as their souls, decayed over time."

Rysanna turned her gaze back on them and let out a shuddering breath. Tears pooled in her eyes, but they remained trapped. "We had no choice. Liliana could not be reasoned with. Her creations attacked our children on her command, killing them with their dark poison."

"It was right of you to end her, my lady," Alak said. "You did end her, did you not?"

Rysanna nodded. "My sister and I vanquished her and her creations, or at least we thought we did. Some of her dark magic lingered over centuries, it seems, as we have discovered with Frederych and the dark artifacts creeping up as of late. We assumed there were followers of this magic and groups of Dark Fae being corrupted by it, but we also began questioning whether they also followed *someone*."

"You think your sister is behind all of this? That she survived somehow?" Katrina asked.

"I can't be sure. When I felt the departure of my High Dorum into the Shadow Realm, it made me even more suspicious. If she somehow managed to cling to that realm, to wield its power instead of suffering from it, it's quite possible she survived." She gestured toward the prone figure. "He called my name in desperation, but when I pulled him from his madness, and he had a moment of lucidity, he remained loyal to who I deciphered from his ravings was his master. His Dark Furae, he had called her. He would give me nothing else."

"So they do have a leader," Aeron acknowledged. "We know that for sure now at least."

"And you really think it could be *her*, dear sister?"

All four of them turned toward the fire and saw the Goddess Allyria standing there in her flowing gown, her head, neck, and wrists adorned with jewels. Unlike Rysanna's natural appearance, the Light Fae sister was dressed for a ball or perhaps even a coronation, with her face perfectly made up. Aeron had only laid eyes on her once before when he and Alak had needed guidance years ago and they called to their Goddess while she and her sister had been visiting.

Allyria practically glided toward them, her face just as pained as her sister's.

Katrina shook her head in disbelief. "Look, if we

have to do battle with a freakin' Goddess now, you need to cure my mate so that we're ready. This entire situation is turning into a shit-show, and I won't have him fighting until he's one hundred percent. So you two need to do *whatever*," Kat whirled her hand in the air like she was holding a wand, "it is that you *do*, and fix him."

Aaron couldn't help but smile at his mate's fierceness. Even in the face of two divine beings, she still put him first. She was exceptional, and he could tell from the look on their Goddess's face that Katrina's protectiveness had won over her approval.

"Please," Katrina begged. "He's in so much pain."

"We need the power of Light and Dark combined," Rysanna stated. "The poison is far more powerful than the previous version we've encountered."

"How so?" Aeron had to ask, especially since those had been his earlier thoughts as well.

"This Dark Furae has found a way to corrupt Light magic as well."

Aeron and Alak both gasped while Allyria shook her head, her eyes gleaming with sadness.

"Your body did not have time to recover as quickly from its weakened state in the Shadow Realm. The creature carried and poisoned you with this new, more potent magic."

"She'd want to be more powerful than both of us this time," Allyria whispered right before she and her sister each placed a hand, one on top of the other, over his wound.

A blinding white glow emanated from within them, filling the entire room and causing him to have to shut his eyes. His scream died in his throat as he was then plunged into darkness. He felt himself gasping for air, and he felt pressure holding him in place. Aeron soon realized it was his brother and his mate keeping him from flailing around. He heard both Alak and Katrina, pleading for him to stay with them and it made him fight harder through the darkness.

Aeron had no idea how much time had passed before he resurfaced, but when he did, he felt whole again and a fierce determination set in to destroy this new threat, no matter how powerful it may be, Goddess or not.

Both Alak and Katrina hugged him tightly. "Don't you ever do that to us again," his mate chided while her face was buried against his neck.

Aeron looked around the room to find Allyria had already gone, the figure on the floor along with her. Rysanna was once again seated opposite them on the other couch.

"I could not have wished for a better mate for my High Dorum," Rysanna said addressing Katrina. "I see a loyalty and strength in you that matches them completely. Go and rest now, my children. Know that you will not be fighting this battle alone. My sister and I have much to make up for."

Aeron stood from the couch with his full strength now returned, Alak and their mate beside him, and he focused on home. Their home. The one that he and his brother would share with their beautiful cougar who had the fire of a dragon. He had already forgiven his Goddess, for even she was not infallible. There was a long, bloody battle looming on the horizon, but for now, even though it would be brief, he wanted to savor a few moments of rest with his brother and his mate by his side.

Chapter Nineteen

As soon as they returned to the garden, Aeron stood and held his hand out for Katrina. She didn't just take his offered hand, she leapt at him, confident he would catch her, and he did not let her down. Her only concern was to get as close to her mates as possible. She wrapped her legs around Aeron's firm waist, settling her arms on his broad shoulders before she buried her fingers in the thick waves of his hair, and claimed his mouth with her own. The fact that he allowed her to control the kiss, to exorcize the demons that had plagued her since she watched him weaken beneath the onslaught of the poison that rocked his system, showed how attuned to her distress he had been.

When she pulled back slightly, to rest her forehead against his, she breathed deeply, taking his scent right into the heart of her, and she shuddered against him in relief.

"I was really scared," she whispered, trusting him with a side of her nature she had never shared with another soul. Not even her Alpha. Fear was not something anyone associated with Braxas's second. The way Aeron's arms tightened around her told Kat that he understood what that admission cost her.

"I know, my love," he said, his voice soft. His hand shook slightly when he reached up to sweep her hair from her face. "It pained me to see you distressed. If I could have spared you that, I would have."

Kat was already shaking her head. "No. This, you, me, and Alak, everything that we are and can be to each other is inextricably linked. I have to know everything that you are feeling, and I sure as hell want to be there when you are hurt. Just as I know you will both be there for me when I get hurt."

She felt and heard Alak's growl of displeasure as he pressed against her back. "It will displease me greatly to see you hurt, dragon."

Kat smiled at the way her mate talked. So otherworldly and outdated, but so damn sexy.

"If Aeron and I were to witness your pain, we would not take it as calmly as you did ours."

Kat reached back to grip the back of Alak's head as he pressed an open-mouthed kiss to the side of her neck. "I'm not sure about how damn calm I was. I yelled at your Goddess, and if she were able to read my mind, then she would have known I was promising bodily harm if she and her sister had not been able to heal Aeron."

Aeron laughed and Kat reveled in the sound. "She would have simply been pleased that our mate is as loving as she is fierce. Something that I for one found extremely arousing."

Kat grinned. "Really?"

"Oh, most definitely."

"A possessive streak is hot as fuck in a mate—as I believe the expression goes?" Alak pressed closer, his teeth closing against the side of her neck for a brief moment, driving a hard spike of arousal through her entire body. "Something I am sure you will come to agree with us on … eventually."

Kat was practically panting, every fiber of her being calling out for the two men who held her between them. "Not so sure about that, my mate. But I am sure on this one thing. I want you. Both of you, and if you don't take me now, then you are going to have one pissed off cougar on your hands and deal with the cost of the damages my cat is likely to do to your beautiful garden."

"*Our* garden," Aeron corrected.

"Right," she said. They hadn't exactly discussed

future plans yet, but she knew her home was wherever her mates were, and the three of them certainly would be cramped in her studio apartment. She couldn't care less about living arrangements at the moment, however.

Kat gasped when she felt the world suddenly shift around her, and found herself lying in the middle of the large, king-sized bed. Naked. As were her mates.

"Wow," she exhaled slowly. "Now that's a handy power to have." The covers were crumpled at the foot of the bed, and the sheets beneath her felt softer than the softest silk. She very much doubted there was a thread count in the Earth realm that could match it.

She took another deep breath, trying to get her equilibrium back, but her men took that moment to put their mouths on her body and all thought of calming down went out the window. She couldn't hold back, crying out in pleasure as Alak took to her left breast, while Aeron went to work on her right, both men using their tongues, teeth, and just the right amount of suction to have her arching up off the mattress.

Mindless with the sensations racing through her body, Kat threw her hands above her head and gave herself over to the pleasure. She inhaled sharply as Alak began to lick and nibble his way down her torso and then shivered with anticipation, her thighs falling apart as he settled between them. She cried out his name when his mouth moved without hesitation to her pussy. The sweep of his tongue and the slight suction he applied to her clit had her rolling her hips against his lips and sobbing in need.

"Goddess," Alak growled, and the vibrations of his voice against her sensitive skin had her quivering, pulsing on the edge of a massive release. "The taste of you is so addictive. I want nothing more than to take you over the edge and into the maelstrom of pleasure, to feel your beautiful pussy quivering against my tongue."

Kat groaned at the sensual picture he painted. She was more than ready for that.

"But I want you too much," Alak finished.

Kat squealed as Alak moved—so fast she could have easily thought he was a shifter—to stand at the foot of the bed. He dragged her along the mattress, not stopping until he had her up and in his arms.

"You are so beautiful, my dragon,"

Kat sighed at his words and the soft expression on his handsome face.

She held onto him, drowning in the intensity of his gaze as he turned to sit on the foot of the bed. When he was completely seated, she lifted up onto her knees and straddled his lap before reaching below her to take the hard length of his erection in her hand.

"I think you're both pretty beautiful, too," she murmured as she shuffled forward, and placed the head of his cock against the slick heat of her pussy. "I have a feeling I'll be fighting the women off of you in both realms."

Alak grinned, and she loved how easily his smile appeared for her. He was her more intense mate, and he certainly hadn't been quick to smile when they'd first met. He made her heart swell with love.

"That evokes some seriously arousing images, Lady Katrina," Alak all but drawled.

"I can't tell you how hot it is to watch you when you are in full battle mode," Aeron whispered in her ear from behind her.

Kat felt like the situation was quickly spiraling out of her control, and she desperately wanted to be in control of this moment, if just for a little longer. As soon as she had both of them buried balls deep within her, she knew the swing of power would most definitely be shifted. She moved her hips to take Alak inside her, loving how his eyes darkened as his body joined hers.

With a smile she knew was as wicked as she felt, she rolled her hips in a tight circle, moving down to take him an inch at a time. Kat was mesmerized by the way Alak's throat moved as he swallowed hard, and she felt the clench of his fingers against her hips. It did something to her to know she affected a man as powerful and strong as Alak. Concentrating on his reactions to her movements, she continued to circle her hips slowly, moving further down the steel length of him until she had all he had to give her. Every hard inch of him was finally buried within her.

"Right here," Alak murmured as his arms wrapped more securely around her, pulling her with him as he lay back against the mattress. "This is home for me. When you take me so completely, so selflessly, into that beautiful body of yours, you show me what it is to be loved. What it is to be a mate, and what it is to be home."

Kat felt tears gather in her eyes as she moved her hands to either side of his shoulders. Unable to find the words to tell him that he and Aeron were all that for her and more, she let her body do the talking. Lifting her hips, she began to move up and down his cock, riding the bursts of pleasure that exploded within her every time she took him to the hilt.

She was just starting to lose herself in the rhythm of her movements and the release she could feel building inside her when Aeron swept the palms of his hands down the arch of her back to settle on her ass.

"You are so beautiful, mate," Aeron said with reverence. When his hands lifted from her body, Kat felt a sense of loss so profound it manifested as an ache in her chest. The ache disappeared moments later when he placed his hands back on her.

"This will feel just a little cold, my love."

Kat gasped at the icy feel of the gel Aeron had just used against her back entrance, and she shivered as he worked the lube into the tight ring of muscle of her ass, before breaching it with his fingers, pressing the cool lube further into her body. Logically, she knew exactly what he was doing—preparing her body to take his, and it made complete and utter rational sense for him to do that. But what made no sense at all, and what she hadn't been prepared for, was how wickedly good it felt. With a moan she pushed back against his fingers.

Alak groaned when her body suddenly tightened around his cock like a vise grip. "It would appear our mate loves to have her ass played with, brother. She is squeezing me so beautifully, her pussy going soft and wet against me. If there is to be any hope of me holding out long enough for you to get inside her so, she can experience what it is to have us both at the same time, then you are going to have to hurry the fuck up. Please. For the love of the Goddess!"

Katrina wanted to echo her own plea for that to happen, too, but nearly all ability to speak was lost to her when Aeron removed his fingers. "No…"

"Shh, Katrina," Aeron crooned as he pressed closer to her, the soothing warmth of his muscular chest pressing against her back. "I'm here, take me."

Kat inhaled sharply when she felt the blunt head of his cock press against her back entrance.

"Push out against me as I push forward, my love."

Kat concentrated on doing what Aeron asked, allowing her back to arch and her body to soften.

"That's it … that's perfect."

She let out a shaky breath as Aeron's cock slid inside and the most delicious feeling of fullness erupted within her. "So full."

"Fuck, mate." Aeron's strained growl erupted behind her, and she could feel the vibration of his voice through her back. "You feel too good. I—I won't be able to last long."

Kat whimpered when he pulled back at the same time as Alak, both of them withdrawing then pushing back into her, the simultaneous sensations driving her arousal to greater heights. She could sense the orgasm building within her and reaching epic proportions, but she held on, determined that she would not go over into that abyss without Alak and Aeron beside her.

"Then don't hold back," she managed to get out in a rush of air. "Fuck me. Please!

Both men took her at her word and began to move within her. At first, they maintained that synchronized movement, but the pleasure was building and soon became too much for either of them to maintain such a steady rhythm. It was not long until they were both slamming into her in jerky movements.

Kat cried out as the tidal wave of her release hovered just beyond her reach. Just as she was about to scream in frustration, she felt Alak slide his hand down her stomach toward her clit. One touch, one swipe of his finger against the swollen nub, was all it took to push her over the edge.

Kat threw back her head and screamed her release to the room. She had no control of the violent shudders that wracked her body as she rode wave after wave of pulsating pleasure. She was vaguely aware of both her men tensing against her, then roaring her name almost in unison, but her triumph at that was short lived as their release triggered another round of tiny explosions within her and she gave herself over to the power of what it was to be loved by them both at the same time.

Chapter Twenty

"What have you two imbeciles done now?"

The voice was deep and rough, causing Zayden's hackles to rise, sensing the threat Dark Furae was to any being around her. She stood in the shadows, a long dark cloak always keeping her hidden. When she had first appeared to him and Nyx, Zayden had wondered what kind of female wielded the powers that she did, but they had both learned very quickly that the less her servants knew, the longer they lasted, and Zayden was determined to be the last man standing at the end of this war.

"There was an unfortunate complication, Mistress," he answered simply.

"Yes, I would say so," she hissed back. "One of my markets was destroyed! Someone shall pay for this. You know I don't like it when others touch what is mine."

"Nyx miscalculated the depravity of his own kind. The hyena Alpha must have led the Dark Fae to the gate's location." Zayden didn't even flinch when the asshole beside him growled low in response to being thrown under the bus, but he wasn't going to be the one paying the price for his partner's fuck up. Shifters high in ambition and low in intelligence were a dime a dozen. The hyena would be easy to replace if it came to that, and he was much more concerned with keeping his own hide intact.

"You," the Dark Mistress said casting her shadow toward the hyena, "you will take care of these Dark Fae permanently … or *I* will take care of *you*. Am I clear?"

"But they have powers, Mistress. How will I take them unawares?" Nyx whined and sputtered.

Furae's irritation was practically a tangible thing,

and Zayden found himself taking a step away from the other male just in case her infamous temper snapped.

"I shall take care of delivering them to you. Make sure you finish the job."

Her last words echoed in the air like a sharp hiss even though Zayden could no longer see her.

****

Alak looked over at Katrina as she lay soundly sleeping in between himself and his brother, happy for this minor reprieve before having to go back to Gabe and Braxas to share what their Goddess had told them. He and Aeron had built their house with their bare hands long ago, and the room they were currently occupying was specifically designed for them to share with their mate, despite the hope of ever finding one having grown bleak. It was almost shocking to Alak when he realized how much their lives had changed in such a short span of time.

It was no longer Alak and Aeron alone to battle the forces that would seek to harm their Goddess or their people. They now had more allies than they could ever have imagined, from two different realms, but most importantly, they had their mate. Suddenly everything they had sacrificed and fought for over the years finally made sense. Every hardship was worth the incredible woman who he held in his arms.

"I can almost *hear* you thinking, Alak," Katrina said, her sexy voice muffled against his chest.

"I'm simply thinking about how I want to stay here all day in bed with you," he replied, running his fingers through the golden locks spread out on the pillow beside her head. Alak had never seen her this relaxed before. She looked ... happy, and even more so because of that, he was loath to return to the real world where they had a war brewing. "This is the first time that I've wanted the rest of the world to just go away for a while."

Katrina lifted her head to look at him and gave him a breathtaking smile. Alak was quickly becoming addicted to the side of her she shared with him and Aeron alone. With everyone else, including her Alpha, she remained serious, a pillar of strength. He loved that about her, but it reached him deep down in his soul that she now trusted her mates with this softer side of herself. When the three of them were together like this, she was not a Beta and he and Aeron were not the Goddess's High Dorum. They were simply men together with the woman they loved.

"I wish that we could." She reached up and gently cupped his cheek in her palm. "But Braxas will be expecting an update from me on what happened, and I don't want to leave them worried about how Aeron's doing. We also have so much to tell them about this possible third Goddess situation."

Aeron sighed. "You are right, of course, but let it be noted that for once, I, too, wish to stay in bed all day."

Katrina giggled. "Noted. I'll just jump in the shower before you two whip us up one of those portals back to Gabe's."

Alak's eyes remained glued to Katrina's breasts as she bounced off the bed and stood. His cock was already half hard thinking about all the things he wanted to do to her under the spray of hot water. "That's a wonderful idea. I think we could all use a shower…"

Her laughter only made him harder as she shook her head and gently pushed him back onto the bed when he tried to follow her.

"Un-uh, you two." She winked. "If you get into that shower with me then you know we won't be making it to the pack house anytime soon."

She gave them a delightful and torturous view of her gorgeous derrière when she turned and walked toward the en-suite bathroom.

"Mischievous wench," he teased as she shut the door behind her.

By the time Katrina was ready to go, Alak and Aeron had used their magic to get clean instead of waiting for their turn in the bathroom. Katrina had been right. There was no more time to waste. The entire shifter community was in danger from this rogue Goddess, and they had their duty to protect them all.

The three of them stood in the kitchen as he and Aeron created the portal, and then they stepped through together, Katrina's hands firmly entwined with theirs. He was pleased that traveling via portal was becoming easier for his mate now, allowing for fewer after-effects. He hated seeing her discomfort. Mere seconds later, after having this thought, something strange happened. He felt an odd, dark magic taking hold of their portal, the likes of which he'd never experienced before. The magic seeped into his very bones, making him feel as if he were suffocating, and it was as if a dark film was creeping over his entire body. He could feel Aeron's magic battling with this unknown source, and the metaphysical blowback when his brother was overpowered was significant, causing all three of them to groan in pain. When the portal opened up, and they were violently spit out, it was not the familiar dense forest outside of Gabe's property they saw, but an empty field. He thanked the Goddess that they were in the human realm at least, and not somehow brought into the Shadow Realm.

Alak grabbed his chest as he writhed on the floor, making sure he was in one piece. His body felt as though it had been torn apart and put back together like a child's puzzle and his head was pounding. The soft groan from beside him brought him back to his senses in a hurry, and he quickly crawled over to where his brother and mate lay, in much the same state as he was.

"Are you all right?" Aeron asked Katrina. She sat with her head cradled in her hands.

"What happened?" she whispered. "I feel like I've been hit by a freight train."

"I … I don't know." Aeron glanced up at Alak. "I think someone took over the portal travel. It should not be possible, but that's the only explanation I can think of."

"I agree, brother. There was definitely another power present, and it was not our Lady Rysanna's."

Maniacal laughter rang out from the other side of the clearing, causing the three of them to jerk their heads in that direction.

"Finally, you have arrived," the hyena bellowed from where he stood, flanked on each side by an Underfae monstrosity. Both of the huge beasts looked ready to kill. "I've waited what seems like forever to get some alone time with you, my pretty kitty. The last time you were in my tender care I didn't get the chance to really show you all of my skills. Once my friends here have taken care of your boyfriends, then you and I will have a party of our own before I end you."

Chapter Twenty-One

Everything within Katrina stilled as her mind became a chaotic swirl of emotion that would have brought her to her knees had she not already been on the ground. Memories of being bound, held in a pair of handcuffs that kept her from shifting, flooded her mind. She had never felt so helpless in her life. She could sense her cougar's displeasure at being shackled in her human form and shared her fear that the move would be permanent. She'd gone to some dark places in those moments. What would become of her if she were unable to allow her cougar, an animal that thrived on freedom and was more dominant than most, an opportunity to be in control? The only answer she came to was madness, an insanity that would eventually cause her to take her own life, or to push Braxas into a position where he would have to put her down. There would have been no other option.

Then, in those dark moments of despair, while she'd experienced vulnerability and doubt in her ability to survive that kidnapping, Nyx had taken advantage of her state of mind. He'd put his hands on her, touching her in a way no man should ever touch a woman without invitation. And he'd fucking enjoyed the way she had cursed and yelled at him, but what really made her sick, what had her entire body turning predator still, was that this bastard had made her feel small and powerless. She had, in the long nights since that attack, experienced nightmares because of him, and she had promised herself that if she were to ever have the opportunity to introduce her cougar to that prick, she would let her dine on his flesh.

"Katrina," Aeron said, his voice low and filled with anger. "This abomination who stands between the two Underfae, is one of the men who hurt you. He dies today."

Kat rose to her feet in one graceful, sensual move, one that was more feline than human. "Yes, he does."

Aeron narrowed his gaze in Nyx's direction then growled. "His master must have placed some kind of magical inhibitor on this place. I cannot reach out with my powers."

"Me neither," Alak said through gritted teeth. "But I could kill him with my bare hands. I want to rip the skin from his body, shred every muscle, tendon and ligament within him, and then force feed him his own internal organs."

Katrina, who until that moment had been locked in a staring contest with the grinning hyena across the clearing, turned to look at her mate with a pointed look. "Man, Alak. You certainly do have a bloodthirsty streak in you a mile wide, huh?"

Alak grinned back at her. "That I do, my dragon, as does my brother."

Aeron turned to look at her. "That's why the Goddess and the Fates have paired us with you, my love. Alak and I would fight every battle, slay all your enemies, and ensure you were never hurt again if you were to allow it, but," Aeron continued, holding his hand up to halt her immediate response to that ancient ethos, "that is not who you are, and it is not what we are as a fated triad. Therefore, we will leave that truly abominable hyena scourge to you, and Alak and I will deal with the unnatural beasts he has brought with him."

Kat frowned and turned back to look in Nyx's direction. Her concentration had been completely locked on the shifter, and she had failed to really take note of the beings—she used that term loosely—who stood at his sides.

"Ewww, those things look like they're decomposing. And that damn stench again…" She shook her head. She'd nearly lost Aeron to one of those things.

As if sensing the direction of her thoughts, Aeron placed his hand on her shoulder and gently squeezed. "We may not have use of our powers, but we are at full strength with the advantage of knowledge now."

"Leave them to us, Katrina." There was no missing the deadly intent in her mate's voice. "You concentrate on making that hyena scream."

Kat's cougar chuffed with pleasure, and she felt a wave of bloodlust roll through her at the thought. She took one step forward then looked back over her shoulder at her mates. "Oh, he'll scream, my loves. I promise you that." She gave both her mates a saucy wink. "Now, last one to kill their evil dance partner over there has to bring me breakfast in bed for a month."

She knew her mates would immediately catch her implication, that there would be no way in hell that she would be last, and saw it in the flicker of amusement that crossed their handsome faces. Then, turning she leapt forward, exploding into her cougar as she went. It was an ability only the most skilled of her kind could ever master. To change whilst in midair and land running on all fours was a difficult one to master, and a skill she had spent many months perfecting. Now she used it to impress upon her enemies that they were dealing with a warrior.

She gave her cougar free rein, embracing the joy as she moved across the ground at an intense speed, reveling in the thrill of the chase, and the anticipation of the fight to come. She watched as Nyx ran toward her, his eyes gleaming with a madness as he changed into his animal. Her cougar snarled her intent to the world as she neared her prey, a sound that echoed off the trees and mountains that surrounded the clearing.

The bastard hyena had taken something from her that day, something she hadn't even known she could lose. He had taken her animal from her, and with that, he had taken a small piece of who she was at the same time. Despite the fact that once the handcuffs were removed she was immediately able to sense her cougar, and knew she hadn't lost her forever, Kat never got that small piece of herself back. Now was the time to rectify that.

And she'd be taking it back bathed in that fucker's blood.

The two animals slammed into each other. Kat used her powerful back legs and flexible spine to twist up and over the hyena, and swipe her paws along both his flanks, reveling in the scent of coppery blood that burst into the air at her move. Landing on all fours, aware of the sounds of battle exploding all around her as her mates joined the fight, she dropped into a crouch, hissing at Nyx and waiting for his move.

Hyenas usually fought as a pack, tending to herd their prey, attacking them in waves until they were eventually able to bring them down and overpower them. On his own, she knew that Nyx would attempt to use brute strength and aggression against her. She would wait for him to come at her, getting in as many swipes as she could, bleeding him until he made a fatal mistake and left his throat exposed. Then she was going to rip it out.

She and Nyx fought like that for a while, both of them getting in a few good hits, both of them bleeding, but Kat was happy to see that he bled a hell of a lot more than she did. Breathing heavily, she stalked to the side, watching and waiting for her enemy's next move.

Which turned out to be the mistake she was

waiting for. Nyx charged, and Kat bunched her muscles in preparation. When the hyena stretched, reaching to grab her flank in his jaws, she struck, using every ounce of preternatural speed she had to launch herself up and twist, to bring her body out of harm's way. Despite her speed, she felt the slice of teeth against her flank that told her Nyx had almost caught her. But it was too late for him. His neck was stretched out right before her, and she was able to clamp her jaws around that vulnerable area, and bite down.

Nxy went wild, scrambling, screaming his displeasure, twisting and raking her with his sharp claws in an attempt to dislodge her and save his worthless life. But it was too little, too late. She bit down, again and again, the bitter taste of his blood filling her mouth, but she refused to let go. She continued to apply pressure even after Nyx seemed to submit to the inevitable, slumping to the ground so that she was able to maneuver her body over his, guarding her prey. She continued to hold on even after she suspected he had taken his last breath.

She only let go when she heard Aeron grunt and turned quickly to make sure he was okay. He had just dispatched his Underfae and had dropped the big bastard to the ground, and a quick check told her that Alak was close to killing his—the beast was missing both his arms. Alak charged the behemoth, and in a lighting quick move, he flipped over him. When he landed on the ground in a graceful crouch, Kat saw that he held the decapitated head of the Underfae. He tossed it aside as he stood up.

Aeron suddenly whirled, muttering words she had no idea what they meant, but from the tone he used and the expression on his handsome face, she figured he was cursing at something in the distance behind her.

When she turned her head to look in that direction, she would have cursed, too, if she could in her human form. Apparently, Nyx and his two little friends hadn't come alone. Seven more Underfae moved out of the forest and in their direction.

"It would appear their master decided to send reinforcements," Alak growled as he moved to stand at Kat's left side, Aeron immediately taking her right. This was going to get ugly, and the odds were not in their favor, but by the Gods she was going to fight with everything in her to end these bastards.

All three of them turned at the explosion of light to the left of their position, and Kat couldn't tell who was more shocked, her and her mates, or the seven bastards who ground to a halt when a wave of cougars and wolves burst into the clearing. It would seem that Dark Furae wasn't the only Goddess getting her portal on at this battle. Her pard and the Vancouver Pack had come to swing the odds completely in their favor.

The fight was over before it even started. Before Kat, Alak, and Aeron had time to step into the newly formed fray, the wolves and cougars had surrounded and trapped the enemy. Katrina, still filled with bloodlust, relished the sounds of tearing flesh and quickly cut-off cries of pain, the shifters all having been schooled on how to quickly dispatch the beasts without coming into contact with their poison. It was done, the enemy defeated … at least for now. And even if the possible other sister-Goddess chose to send more minions, it was clear that the Dark and Light Fae Goddesses would intervene as well.

Kat shifted into her human form and was quickly covered up with Alak's shirt. Unfortunately, she had no time to ogle her mate's naked chest due to the fact that a lone figure in the far-off distance caught her attention. He was definitely Underfae, though not as large as the corrupted bear-like beasts. He looked more like he was once a Dark Fae man. He inclined his head and stared at her and then at the scene before him. He seemed curious, but something about him felt non-threatening, at least toward their group at the moment.

He simply nodded, then turned and walked away.

"Did you see that?" she asked her mates.

Aeron nodded. "I don't think he was with the others."

"And he did not appear to be upset that his kind were defeated," Alak added.

Aeron seemed to ponder for a moment before he spoke. "Perhaps not *all* of our Underfae brothers and sisters are lost to us then. Maybe there is hope to redeem or heal some?"

"One could only hope, brother."

Suddenly, Aeron and Alak gave a slight jerk, causing panic to rise in Katrina, but as if sensing her distress, Aeron gently placed his arm around her and said, "Do not be concerned, love. We just felt the force of whatever Dark Furae put over this area being lifted. Our magic has returned."

"Good," Gabe said, walking over to them in human form. "Now we can get back to the house and start planning how to take this dark bitch down. And we've also got a whole bunch of bears arriving shortly."

With her mates' powers and Aeron's full strength returned, no assistance from the Goddesses was needed to return to the pack house. Aeron and Alak opened up a portal, sending everyone through in groups. Once arrived, Katrina and the twins began swapping information with Gabe, Braxas, and Corrine.

The Goddess Rysanna had come to Corrine in a

vision and told her about Dark Furae being the leader of the Underfae. Alak and Aeron had filled in what was left out in Rysanna's haste to get aid sent to Karina and her men. Gabe and Braxas had been keeping the Alpha of the bears, Booker, in the loop, and it was decided that their presence here was needed if they were to all have a chance of defeating this new and the most dangerous threat Fae and shifter-kind had ever faced.

Shifters, Light and Dark Fae, and even the Goddesses would all have to fight together, for otherwise the world around them would be forever altered by this evil.

"I'm proud of you, Kat," Braxas said, placing his hand on her shoulder. "And honored to have you as my Beta."

Alak and Aeron had beamed with pride as they told her Alpha how bravely and valiantly she had fought and won against one of her former captors.

"At every turn, no matter what was thrown at her, she acted and reacted like a soldier, like a leader," Alak had said.

"Despite how much my brother and I had stubbornly wanted to keep her out of harm's way," Aeron had added. "I think she saved us, too."

The last part was added so quietly, that had it not been for shifter hearing, she was sure no one in the room would have heard it. The truth was, physically, she had healed from all of her wounds, but the mental ones had lingered. She had to fight her own demons and slay them, but she finally realized that she didn't have to do it alone. And she'd won … defeated them all by finding the strength within herself, the strength her mates had helped her find.

Kat had always been brave, brazen even, in the

face of a fight, but she had been scared to face the turmoil inside herself. She even thought herself a coward for it and nearly drowned in the sorrow of her own darkness. Never again. And if there was hope for her, maybe there was hope left for at least some of the enemy like the stranger in the field.

That was a problem for a different day though. She looked around the room at her pard, her pack, and lastly, to her mates and felt hope that they would all be victorious. They had to be. She was finally feeling whole again, and the two men beside her were the loves of her life, something else she never thought she would find. There was no way some jilted, twisted sister was going to take that away from her.

Katrina would never stop fighting for the chance to have forever with her mates.

Epilogue

"Yes! Harder … please, please … harder!"

Aeron looked down at his flushed mate's face and felt his desire swell even more from her sexy pleas. He could not refuse her, and his own body desperately craved release. He took her mouth in a fiery kiss before sitting up on his haunches and shifting her legs over his shoulders in the process. He drove into her, thrusting faster and harder as she requested. Her beautiful round breasts bounced and swayed with the motion until Alak swooped down on them and began lavishing his attention. He couldn't blame his brother. There wasn't an inch on their mate that was not inviting.

Her breasts came into full view again when Alak shifted his position to kneel by Katrina's head. She eagerly took him into her mouth, hollowing in her cheeks and taking him as deep as she could go. Alak sweetly cupped her cheek as she pleasured him. Aeron knew all too well how her plump lips felt around his own cock. She had quickly learned his weak spots and often used it to bring him to his knees, expertly twirling her tongue and sucking him down until he would nearly pass out.

Right now, though, her sweet pussy gripped him tightly. That, along with her deep and sexy moans around his brother's shaft, told him she was close. He wrapped his arms around her legs and continued to plunge in hard, but slowing down his strokes so that he could stay in her depths longer.

Finally, he felt her quiver around him, her legs shook, and then he threw his head back and roared out his own release. As he emptied inside her, he heard Alak call out Katrina's name as if she were a prayer on his lips.

Their mate *was* an answered prayer, he thought, one he never even knew he sent up to the Goddess. Never before had he and Alak ever faced a threat they weren't confident they could eventually defeat or at the very least immobilize, but the Dark Furae, even without her army, was most likely the third Goddess sister, one with forbidden powers, whose poisonous wound needed two powerful Goddesses to heal.

He and Alak collapsed beside their cherished mate, all three sated for the moment. They had everything to lose now and somehow needed to find the strength to make sure they wouldn't. Even the power of a wayward Goddess would not separate the three of them. He vowed it.

"A girl could get used to waking up like this every morning," Katrina said with a smile, her voice still raspy from a combination of sleep and crying out during their activities.

Alak laughed. "So could her men."

"I love you both so much," she said fiercely. Aeron heard the emotion thick in her voice. He'd never tire of hearing her say those words to him.

He'd also never tire of saying them back to her. "As we love you, my dragon." He kissed her lips just as Alak stated his own sentiment to her.

Aeron waggled his brows at Alak. "I believe someone has to go make breakfast."

Katrina giggled as Alak grumbled getting out of bed, and then she burst into hysterics—a sound sweeter than music to his ears—when Alak threw a pillow at the both of them. It wasn't the making breakfast part that had Alak grousing at them, but the fact that Aeron and Katrina kept implying the reason behind it—coming in last with his kill.

Neither he nor Alak minded making their lady

breakfast in bed, though. In fact, when the month was up, he'd look forward to preparing those meals for her as well, just as he had enjoyed their domestic moments of the three of them cooking dinner together these past two weeks. He wondered how he and Alak had ever managed to live without her. She fit seamlessly into their lives, making it far richer than he could have ever dreamed of.

After breakfast, Aeron had graciously offered to clean up while Katrina and Alak showered together. He did, after all, get some extra *quality* time while Alak had prepared breakfast. A soft knock at the door came just as he was finishing up.

"Aneena," he said in greeting, giving his cousin a kiss on the cheek. He stepped aside and motioned for her to come in. "Is everything all right?" He noticed she looked unusually flustered.

"Yes…" She hesitated for a brief moment, as if she wanted to add something else. "Yes. Everything is fine. I'm not disturbing you, am I? I thought I would walk over with you to the council meeting."

Aeron gestured for Aneena to sit down at the dining table, and he sat down beside her, taking her hand in his. "I sense something is troubling you. Please tell me so that I may help."

"N-nothing is troubling me, Aeron. I assure you."

Aeron sighed. "The meeting is tomorrow." He and Alak planned to brief the village on all they had learned with regards to the battle ahead now that they had information. "Is today not your time with the Queen of the Light Fae and her children?"

Aneena blushed, causing Aeron to be even more confused at her disconcerted state. "Lady Eyrica, her mates, and the twins were all in the human realm."

"You know you are most welcome at the pack

house." He was sure Gabe, Braxas, and Corrine would not have minded her doing lessons with the children there.

"Oh, yes. I was there. I just l-left early." Again, a blush bloomed on her cheeks, even deeper this time. "There was too much activity going on … a lot of extra *guests*."

Aeron nodded. He had told Aneena as much weeks ago. They would be fighting this war with many allies on their side. "Was anyone unwelcoming toward you?"

His cousin shook her head slowly. "No. Not at all." She took a deep breath. "There were *bears*…" she trailed off on a whisper.

The End

www.elenakincaid.com

www.maiadylan.com

www.sarahmarshfiction.com

Elena Kincaid, Maia Dylan, and Sarah Marsh

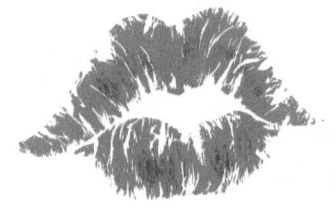

EVERNIGHT PUBLISHING ®

www.evernightpublishing.com